BENT NOT BROKEN
MADELINE AND JUSTIN

Text copyright © 2017 by Lorna Schultz Nicholson
Published by Clockwise Press Inc.,
56 Aurora Heights Dr., Aurora, ON L4G2W7

www.clockwisepress.com
christie@clockwisepress.com   solange@clockwisepress.com
10 9 8 7 6 5 4 3 2 1

Library and Archives Canada Cataloguing in Publication
Schultz Nicholson, Lorna, author
Bent not broken : Madeline and Justin / Lorna Schultz Nicholson.
(One-2-one ; 3)
Issued in print and electronic formats.
ISBN 978-1-988347-03-5 (softcover). ISBN 978-1-988347-04-2 (PDF)
I. Title. II. Series: Schultz Nicholson, Lorna. One-to-one ; 3.
PS8637.C58B46 2017   jC813'.6   C2017-900271-6 .
C2017-900272-4

Design concept by Tanya Montini
Interior and cover design by CommTech Unlimited
Printed in Canada by Webcom

MIX
Paper from
responsible sources
FSC® C004071

BENT NOT BROKEN
MADELINE AND JUSTIN

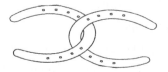

A ONE-2-ONE BOOK

Lorna Schultz Nicholson

CLOCKWISE
PRESS

AUTHOR'S NOTE

The Best Buddies is a real program that operates in schools, including colleges and middle schools, all over the world. Students with intellectual disabilities pair up with volunteer peer "Buddies." They meet together, one-to-one, or at school, at least twice monthly to engage in fun, social interaction. They also participate in group activities, including events like the Evening of Friendship that takes place in this novel. That said, this book is a work of fiction. Justin and Madeline are fictional characters, meaning I made them up. I also made up where they live, their high school, and families and all their situations. I did a tremendous amount of research so I could write the novel but in the end it is a work of fiction. Fiction is pleasure reading. So, please, enjoy!!

To Peggy Lalor.
Your progress is inspiring!
- L.S.N.

CHAPTER ONE
MADELINE

S ometimes I think I should just wear a sign.

I fell off my bike. I hurt my brain.

Words get stuck in my brain. And I talk slowly. I know that. I can almost picture the words and see them first, before they travel to my mouth. I think it's when they start to move that they slow down, like an old train screeching to a stop. Then, when they do come out, the vowels are often long. *Toooo looong.* Again, I know that. I'm not stupid. Seriously. I wish people (mainly kids at school but, well, adults too because they stare) knew that about me as soon as they met me. I wish they could tell by looking at me that I fell off my bike when I was eight and the fall hurt my brain.

But, of course, I would never wear *any such sign* because it would draw even more attention to me and would make me less normal than I already am. In high school it's hard to be not-normal. Whatever normal is.

"Come on Maddie, hurry," Becky called out from the mud room. Becky is my identical twin who didn't fall off her bike but was with me when I fell off mine. "Maddie, did you hear me?"

"Cooooming," I replied.

I entered the mud room, and took my winter parka from the hook, struggling to put it on. My balance is iffy. After my accident I couldn't walk so I had to fall and get up and fall and get up to learn again. My gait is still off a little too. For the record, *gait* is a rehab word. Yes, I did rehab. Like, a lot of trying to walk with walkers and therapy contraptions.

"We can't miss the bus," said Becky, helping me with my coat.

"Yoooou like miiissing the buuus," I said. Becky always understands me no matter how slowly I talk.

"Not today."

I wondered why *not today* although I guess I didn't really want to know.

Becky and I are identical twins, so when stuff changes in her life, it changes in mine too. And that is true for her too. When I suddenly couldn't walk or talk anymore we lost *us*—I lost us, the stupid bike lost us, and we weren't identical anymore. And that was so weird because we had always been a unit: one, not two. We used to be those twins who dressed the same, down to the same yellow butterfly barrettes and days-of-the-week underwear.

As soon as we stepped outside I heard the local bus with its rude belching, as it lumbered down the street. Becky grabbed my hand. "We have to run," she said.

I tried to run but kept stumbling.

"You can do it," she encouraged.

One foot in front of the other. One foot in front of the other. I had to concentrate, make my brain cooperate. Some mornings it took way too much effort.

"Almost there," she said.

Most of the time Becky was happy missing the bus because she could blame it on me and still miss first period. The bus driver waited. Panting, I got on, grabbed the railing, and climbed the two stairs to get to the top.

"You girls should leave your house earlier," said the driver to both of us as we showed him our bus passes. Then he focused on me and smiled. "Good running, though." He winked. He was my favourite driver by far.

I attempted to sit in the first available seat but Becky put her arm around my shoulder. "Let's go to the back," she whispered. The bus lurched forward but Becky held onto me so I wouldn't fall.

With her guidance, we made it to the back and I quickly sat down.

Three stops later, three girls got on. Three loud, obnoxious girls. They made their way to the back. I cringed and looked down at my hands.

"Hey, Beck," Molly called. Last year Molly had blonde hair but now it was dyed black to match her new black wardrobe. Of all Becky's newly acquired friends, Molly was the one who was nicest to me. The other two, Cassandra and Gwinnie, chewed gum and blew bubbles, popping them with a loud, cracking noise. They also wore black, as in black jackets, but they certainly weren't dramatic like Molly, who wore a black velvet cape that she'd bought at Value Village. Becky told me that. Now she wanted to shop there too, when just a year ago she hated anything that was second hand because it smelled. *Like old people*, she had always said.

Cassandra wore a plaid hat and some long feathered, black earrings, while Gwinnie had a red toque with a pom-pom. All three of them wore black eyeliner, which made the white in their eyes look like black-rimmed fluorescent lights. In the hospital I had stared up at those kinds of lights for hours.

"Hey," said Becky. "Saved you seats."

She slid down and they took over the entire back row in the bus. I refused to look at them and kept staring at my hands. They ignored me too, which was fine by me. As they chatted on and on about their weekend, I just sat there, listening. Sometimes my brain jumbles words and I miss some, but since they said *party* so many times, I could get what they were saying. My mother didn't know anything about Becky's new friends. Why Becky had picked them was a mystery to me. Or had they picked her? They didn't pick me, that was for sure, and I was okay with that.

I stared out the bus window at the dirty snow, imagining the green grass and colourful flowers that would sprout soon. Spring is my favourite time of year. Except for the year I fell. It was spring then, and after my accident I was in the hospital for the entire summer. By the time I got out it was fall and I'd missed all of summer vacation. Then I missed an entire year of school. My mother fought to keep me in the same grade as Becky so she made me work from home.

I was enjoying my quiet time, my view, until I smelled the smoke.

Not again.

I turned. "Beeeecky, no, pleeeease," I said.

"Madeline, you seriously need to live a little." Gwinnie laughed. Then she leaned over and blew smoke in my face.

"Dooon't," I said, fanning away the smoke with my hand.

I looked to Becky but she hadn't even noticed what Gwinnie was doing to me because she was too busy sucking on the cigarette, her cheeks hollowed in.

"It's not like it's *drugs* or anything," said Cassandra. Laughing, she blew out a smoke ring.

"Good one," said Gwinnie. She blew out two rings. "Beat ya."

Suddenly, the bus swerved to the side of the road and came to a complete stop. The driver got out of his seat and stood in the aisle to face the passengers. From the front of the bus he yelled, "Girls, off my bus! Now!"

"What a grump," said Gwinnie.

Everyone picked up their backpacks. Becky grabbed the side of my coat and said, "We gotta go."

I crossed my arms over my chest.

"You've got to come with me," Becky whispered.

"Let's go, girls!" yelled the driver.

"Girls means you," said Gwinnie as she walked by me. "You're guilty by association."

"Awww, poor Madeline," mocked Cassandra.

"Shuuut uuup," I said.

"Leave her alone," said Molly, as she stepped out the back doors.

I glared at Becky but she pleaded with her eyes so...I stood. She gently took my arm and walked behind me. I followed Cassandra out the back doors, trying to ignore the stares and mutters from the other passengers.

After we were outside and the bus had pulled away, the girls started laughing.

"Did you see his face?" Cassandra howled.

"He was pissed." Gwinnie pulled out her package of Camel cigarettes and lit one.

"Weee're gonna be...laaaate," I said. I almost had to spit my words. Between the humiliation on the bus and the fact that I was stuck on the side of the road with these morons, I could feel my brain getting worked into a lather.

Lather. My mother's word for my meltdowns. Not a bubble bath. A lather. Words and emotions get jumbled inside me. I wish they felt more like bubbles instead of spewing foam, though. My heart starts beating faster and faster.

Cope, Madeline, cope. Right then, I knew I had to try some of the coping strategies I'd learned from my therapists. And fast. I let my arms fall to my side, like limp noodles. Did it help? My body still shook. *Please, not now.* Not right here. Embarrassment personified.

Please.

Relax. Relax. I opened my mouth, letting my jaw drop.

"We won't be late if we run," said Gwinnie.

Becky glanced my way. "You guys go," she said quickly. "I'll walk with Maddie."

I think she figured out I was starting to panic, lose it, lather up, freak out, have a meltdown, whatever it's called. I get these moments of accelerated heart-racing, heated skin, shaking, and pounding in my head. Also, since the accident, my brain struggles with emotions, as if at times all the wires are crossed; I laugh when I should cry and cry when I should laugh.

I closed my eyes. Becky was the only one I allowed to call me Maddie, and to hear her say it did make me relax a little. I could calm down. I could.

I opened my eyes to see Cassandra, Gwinnie, and Molly running, laughing, squealing. I couldn't have gone with them even if I wanted to. I was a fast runner when I was little, faster than Becky. In elementary school I could even beat the boys. I do have memories of before my accident, just not from the exact day, the fall, the ambulance ride.

"I doooon't…liiike theeem," I said.

"Whatever," she said. "They're my friends not yours." She took my backpack and slung it over her back. "Let's go."

We didn't talk the entire way to the school and I managed to calm down completely, which was a good thing because no one liked me when I threw a fit, especially me. The halls were quiet and empty when we finally arrived at school and our first stop was the office.

"We missed the bus," said Becky.

Mrs. Benoit looked up from her computer and over her funky purple glasses. She glanced quickly at Becky then shifted her gaze to me and as soon as she did she smiled and nodded her head. "Okay, I understand," she said.

"Yeah," said Becky in this syrupy voice that she sometimes used on my mother when she wanted something. "Bus driver just went right by us."

Mrs. Benoit slid two slips across the counter.

Outside the office, I said, "It waaasn't *myyyy* fault. Heee's a niiice driiiver."

Becky shrugged. "Who cares? We're not in trouble. You can get away with missing the bus, but I can't. I can only get away with it when I'm with you."

Becky and I walked to our lockers. They're side by side because my mother insisted. My aide, Mr. Singh, stood by my locker. I hate that I need an aide but I do for certain subjects. My goal is to one day NOT need one.

"We missed the bus," said Becky. "Sorry."

"Did you check in at the office first?" he asked.

Becky handed over my late slip.

"Get your books," he said to me. "We need to get you to math."

Math. My dreaded subject. I hate it more than I hate having an aide assist me. My brain just won't do it. Numbers get jumbled and they bounce. Equations confuse me.

"See you at lunch," said Becky.

I shook my head. "I'm meeeeeting Justiiin," I said.

"Oh right. Best Buddy time. Have fun."

"Mom's piiicking us uuup," I said.

"I know," she rolled her eyes. "We have to go see the *horses*."

"You uuused to liiike them." Going to see the miniature horses is my favourite thing to do. My. Favourite. Thing. To. Do.

"They smell." She scrunched her nose.

"This is a discussion for later," said Mr. Singh. He tapped my locker. "Math books."

Becky slammed her locker shut. "Catch you later," she said. Then she turned her back and walked away from me.

Mr. Singh and I went to my math class, one that is filled with people like me. Other losers who can't do math. We get called a lot of different names: losers, dummies, brain-deads. I think the brain-dead comment is geared toward me.

I slipped in and sat beside Gloria, another girl who is in the Best Buddies program at school. The difference between Gloria and me is that she was born with FAS, (that's fetal alcohol syndrome, meaning her mother drank too much alcohol when she was pregnant with her) so she's always been the way she is, but I was like everyone else until I was eight. I could do math then, well as much math as an eight-year-old can. The funny thing is even after my accident, when I was nine and ten, I could do math. But when it got complicated in junior high school my brain got muddled. And yes, that started another round of testing and doctors' appointments. *Why can't Madeline do math anymore? What is her problem? Why is this happening now? Is this because of the brain damage?*

It sure the heck is.

Gloria leaned over and said, "Hi, Madeline."

"Hiiii," I said back.

"How come you're late?"

I shrugged.

"I'm going to my Best Buddy's for lunch."

"Wiiilla's hooouse?"

Gloria nodded and smiled so all her teeth and her gums showed. "I like Willa," she said. "Do you like Justin?"

"Yeees," I said.

She put her hand to her mouth and giggled. "You like Justin." She sort of sang the words so it came out like I *liked* him.

"He's a hottie," she said. "I'd like to do him."

"He haaas a giiirl-friend," I said. Gloria talked about stuff like boys all the time. It was part of her FAS. Just like speaking slow, having crazy emotions, and being crappy at school was part of my brain damage.

"Do you want to *do* him?" she asked and laughed.

"Nooo," I answered.

"I would." More laughing. Her shrill voice jabbed me like a needle.

I could feel my heart race, my skin prickle, and my brain swirl. No, *please, no*. Gloria's giggling was irritating, grinding against my skull. It hurt. I didn't *like* Justin. I just liked him.

I uncrossed my legs and ankles. I let my shoulders drop. I unclenched my hands. She kept giggling. Why didn't she just stop already? Her voice pounded inside my head, like a hammer hitting the side of my skull. Over and over. Pounding. Pounding. I didn't want her to laugh anymore or take what I said the wrong way. I closed my eyes, tried to breathe, tried to remember everything I was supposed to do, but the hammering wouldn't stop. *Bang. Bang.* And then, like a crack of thunder, I did what I wasn't supposed to.

"Stoooop laaaughing!" My voice boomed as I yelled.

Some kids turned to look at me. That made my heart race even faster as the lather frothed. "Dooon't looook at meee!" I yelled again.

Mr. Singh put his hand on my shoulder. "Are you okay, Madeline?"

I slouched in my seat and stared at the desk. My cheeks burned. My body shook. I tried to breathe but I was gasping. My anger still circled, around and around. Then the end of my fingers started pulsing.

No.

Then it happened.

I started hitting my head with my hand. It hurt. I didn't care. I kept hitting. I wanted it to hurt. And hurt. And hurt. I hated my brain. But I wanted to stop too. But I couldn't stop.

Mr. Singh gently pulled my hand away, holding it by the wrist.

"Let's do some math," he said quietly.

And just like that it was over. I knew my face was red because it burned. I sucked in air, exhaling, and I stared down at the desk, not wanting to look at anyone or see everyone looking at me.

After breathing in and out three times, I nodded. I slowly lifted my head to look at Mr. Singh and I tried to smile. To get everything back to normal, I said, "I haaate maaath."

"I know you do," he said, winking at me. "But let's try, okay? The more we help your brain, the more it helps you."

"Sooorry," I whispered to Gloria.

"It's okay," she replied. She smiled at me, again, teeth showing, and I tried to smile back. I did.

The morning slogged by and, finally, it was time for lunch. I went to my locker, and before opening it I glanced in my pencil case for the numbers to open my lock. Why could I remember being little and riding my bike before my accident, but not my lock combination? Every day I had to look.

Once I put my books away, I checked my schedule that was taped to my locker door before I got my lunch, just to see what I had in the afternoon. Phys-ed. Great. I sucked at phys-ed, even the dance stuff. One-two-three, trip-and-fall. I was worse at gymnastics. I shut my locker door and stared up and down the hall. Becky was nowhere to be seen so I walked to the cafeteria by myself.

Justin met me at the door to the cafeteria and I liked that.

"Hey, Madeline." He held up a pack of cards. Usually we played Go Fish.

I held up my thumb. He cracked a small smile because he wasn't a smiley kind of guy. But happiness sometimes showed up in his eyes and today I could tell he was happy to see me. I liked him because he didn't feel sorry for me; he just liked me. Plus, we didn't have to talk a lot.

We found a table in the corner and I opened my lunch kit and took out a container with quinoa salad. Justin opened his too and he had a piece of leftover pizza. It looked good, better than my mother's boring "healthy diet" salad. *Brain food* she called it.

Justin finished his pizza before I finished my salad, so he took out a deck of cards and started shuffling. The cards flew from one hand to another without spilling.

"How was your weekend?" he asked, shuffling back and forth and then putting the cards together and snapping them in the middle. He grinned at me as he swirled a card around his finger.

"I saaaw the hooorses," I said.

"Horses?" He put the card back in the deck and went back to normal shuffling, but he didn't look at me.

"Miiini hooorses," I said. They were actually miniature horses but that was a hard word for me to say.

He kept shuffling and shuffling but he still didn't look at me. Something was wrong. Was he scared of horses? Should I try and say miniature?

"Theeey're liiittle," I said.

He lifted his head and smiled at me but this time it wasn't a real smile, not like before.

"I'll deal seven cards, okay? he said.

"I waaalk them," I said. "And giiive theeem treeeats."

Justin laid out seven cards for each of us. I put my salad container away in my lunch kit, wiped my hands with a sanitary wipe, and picked up my cards. I stared at all the suits before I arranged them. I could do this. Yes, I could. Go Fish was a good game for me.

"You go first," said Justin.

I had to concentrate, move the cards in my hand, look for more than one of the same kind, and put them together. Once I had my hand organized I looked at it again. I had put two tens together.

"Dooo you haaave a teeen?" I asked.

He pulled a ten dollar bill out of his pocket. "I sure do."

I laughed.

We were on our second game when Becky walked by with her friends. They were laughing at something on Cassandra's phone.

"Beeecky," I called out.

She turned, gave me a little wave and a blown kiss, but kept following her friends. I wanted her to come over and see me with Justin, talk to him, or talk to me. But she didn't. She kept walking with her friends.

I felt tears starting to prickle behind my eyes, so I closed them and thought of the horses. In my mind I tried to smell the hay, feel Willow's coarse mane in my fingers, and hear her hooves on the ground and the whinny of her voice as she talked to me.

"Hey, it's okay," said Justin. "Let's play another game."

I opened my eyes. "I waaant *you*...to cooome see the...hooorses with meee," I said. "I'm goooing tonight."

CHAPTER TWO
JUSTIN

Horses?

For a brief time, minutes perhaps, Madeline had allowed me to forget what day it was. But the word "horses" made the protective bubble around my heart burst and that stabbing pain returned.

"Um," I said to Madeline. "I'm not sure about that." I shuffled the cards, making noise. Why did she ask me this today? I tried to focus on the flipping cards and not on what I was thinking. I hadn't seen or touched a real horse since my younger sister Faith died. She and I used to go to the barn all the time to brush their hair, braid their manes, and give them apples. And Faith loved to mount the slowest horse and be walked around and around the stable. Yes, I knew Madeline did horse therapy at the ranch with miniature horses but…go with her?

Madeline didn't say anything but I could tell by the downward turn on her face she was confused, even hurt.

After what her sister had just done to her, treating her like she was garbage with those new friends of hers, I wanted to say yes, I really did, but the words wouldn't come out of my mouth. I wondered if that's how Madeline felt *all the time*; that words just wouldn't come out. The fall off her bike had made her brain into scrambled eggs. That's how it was described to me by Mrs. Beddington when she'd put us together as Best Buddies. Like the wires in her brain had gotten all mixed up. But Madeline was still working on putting them back in order.

Answer her.

"Um," I said. What was I thinking? How could I turn her down? What kind of Best Buddy was I? Here I was, the Chapter President of the Best Buddies in our school, and I couldn't even say I would go see some little horses with *my* Best Buddy?

Say something, Justin.

I took a deep breath before I said, "Okay. Maybe one day." I glanced at my phone to see the time. "We're good for one more game. How about we switch it up and play War?"

"I'm gooood at Waaar," she said. "I beat Beeecky."

Suddenly, her smile disappeared. She was obviously still stinging from Becky's actions or lack of actions. I performed another card trick. Faith had loved my card tricks. After pulling the Queen of Hearts out of Madeline's ear, I said, "You go first," in the liveliest voice I could muster.

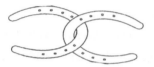

When school was over for the day, I made my way to the bus stop. My girlfriend, Anna, sometimes drove me but today I wanted to be alone.

What awaited me at home? I shivered under my hoodie. Why the heck didn't I wear a coat?

Everything will be okay. I checked my phone for a text message from my father. Nothing. This was a good thing.

As I stepped on the bus, I yanked my bus pass out of my backpack and in the process dropped a photo onto the dirty bus floor. I looked down to see Faith hugging a horse.

"Move it," said a man behind me.

I quickly picked up the photo, wiped the dirt off it, and made my way to the middle of the bus. Without looking at the photo again, I shoved it back in the plastic folder with my bus pass. Usually I had it stashed deep but this morning I'd taken it out to look at it. I needed her near me today.

As the bus barrelled along, I played with the ties on my backpack, a feeling of dread pressing on my shoulders. The bus stopped and lurched forward, stopped and lurched forward again, over and over. One stop. Two stops. And so on and so on. Every time the doors opened I wanted to jump off and run somewhere, anywhere that was in the opposite direction of my home.

Finally. My stop. I got off the bus and my stomach tied into knots. I walked the block to my home and when I got there, I stood on the sidewalk out front and stared at our brick house. Dark. It was so dark. Not one light was on.

Strange.

I walked up the driveway to the garage and punched in the code. The door screeched as it opened. Only my mother's car was parked, the same dust on the windshield from weeks ago. My dad's car was gone. *Where was he?* We'd made a deal. I was supposed to go to school because I had a test and he was supposed to take the day off and spend it with my mom. Again, the dread pressed on my shoulders, the weight almost buckling my knees.

Where was he?

Maybe my mom had gone with him somewhere?

I inhaled and exhaled then walked outside again. I shut the garage. Then I leaned up against the house, the cold brick pressed against my cheek, and tried to breathe. Okay, this was ridiculous. I was probably over-reacting.

Just go in the house, Justin. Stop stalling.

I started walking up the front walk, slowly. My dad would have texted me if something was wrong. Of course he would have. But he probably would have sent a text telling me they were going out too.

The front door was unlocked so I pushed it open and listened. Not a sound, except the ticking grandfather clock in our hallway, heat blasting through the vents, and my heart beating. Or should I say pounding. My skin had turned clammy and slimy, and it wasn't because of a flu bug. I stepped inside and dropped my backpack on a bench, the thudding sound echoed through the front lobby.

The house felt lifeless.

"Dad," I called out.

No answer.

Since there was no light on in the kitchen, or anywhere downstairs, I slipped out of my shoes and padded toward the stairs. I wiped my hands on my pants and went up. When I came to the master bedroom door, I stopped and put my ear to the door. No noise. No movement.

No breathing.

I pressed my forehead against the wooden door. I heard the furnace kick in. A light bulb hiss. Cars outside. I rapped lightly on the door with my knuckles.

Nothing.

"Mom," I said quietly.

Again. No answer. Was she in there? Or somewhere with my dad?

My dad and I took turns keeping an eye on Mom, especially when she was having a particularly bad time of things. Like today. The anniversary of Faith's death. She'd been gone for a whole year.

I slowly pushed open the door and saw the lump under the duvet. I walked over to the bed, the carpeted floor absorbing my footsteps. Once I was at the side, I stared down, and a wave of relief washed over me when I saw the little flutter of her eyes. I fell to my knees in front of her and pushed greasy, damp strands of hair off her cheeks.

"Mom," I whispered. "I'm here. I'm home now."

Her eyes flickered again before settling, into her deep darkness. It was okay. She was alive, breathing, and that was a good thing.

"Everything is going to be okay," I said. "We just need to get through today."

More eye movement. A tiny twitch. My lips curled up in a tiny smile. I was relieved. Really relieved. I sat down with my back against her bed. How many times had I done this? Talked to her knowing the conversation would be one-sided. Talked about anything. Just talked. Too many to count but it did help. Well, it helped me anyway.

"I want to tell you about Madeline," I started. I didn't wait for her to answer me because the truth was she probably wouldn't. Not right now. Maybe later. That was okay. Sometimes I talked for an hour without her waking up, just nattered on and on.

"She's really sweet," I said. "She kind of looks like Faith. Just a little. She has dirty-blonde hair and that wave Faith had in hers. Faith's was a little lighter though. And she has brown eyes like Faith. Remember how beautiful Faith's eyes were when she laughed? Oh, and Madeline has a sister, an identical twin but you can tell them apart by how they dress and, well, Madeline's brain damage." I stopped talking for a few seconds and stared at the taupe-painted wall in front of me. "Now, that's a big difference. Faith only had me, a brother."

I tapped my fingers together for a few seconds, waiting to see if I would get some sort of answer. None. Not even a peep.

I ran my hand through my hair. But then I started talking again. "Being with Madeline makes me think of Faith. The brain is so complicated. Look at Faith. She was so brilliant at so many things. Remember how fast she could do Sudoku puzzles? Or that Rubik's cube." I laughed and turned slightly to glance at my mom to see if she was waking up with these memories, but no go.

"Madeline is smart too. And a real fighter. She's done so much therapy. Speech therapy, physical therapy, occupational therapy, and everything else to help put her life back together as best she can. Therapy's good, Mom."

I glanced at her out of the corner of my eye. We'd been trying to get my mother to go back to therapy. Unsuccessfully.

I turned away from her again and continued talking. "But Madeline wasn't born with hers, like Faith was. From what Mrs. Beddington told me—remember Mrs. Beddington, Mom? She always asks about you—anyway, Mrs. Beddington told me that it took Madeline over a year to learn to walk again. Now her brain sometimes can't do what she wants it to. But I might have told you this already." I paused for a second. "Faith's autism locked her thoughts in her mind too. That's what I think. We need to remember the good things, Mom. Remember how Faith liked food shows? She'd watch them for hours. Oh, and horses. It was like she could speak to them by touching them. She would have made a good horse whisperer. That's something she could have done."

I stopped my babbling. I had to. Perhaps I'd gone too far today, talking about Faith and the things she *could have* done. I closed my eyes for a second and then my stomach growled. Enough. Obviously I wasn't getting through.

I stood and started to gather my things.

"She would have been fourteen already," whispered my mom.

The sound of her scratchy voice made me sit on the bed. "You're awake." I took the glass of water from her nightstand. "Are you thirsty?"

"She didn't even get to be fourteen," she said. "I...I...should have...I should have spent every minute with her."

"It wasn't your fault."

"Yes...it was. I put her in that place. She hated it. It killed her. I killed her."

My parents had decided to put Faith in a rehab program for girls with eating disorders. It hadn't worked. She'd just learned new tricks. "No, Mom. Those kids at her school. They made her hate herself."

"I should have brought her home when she begged. She fooled everyone. She was so smart."

"Shhh." I put my hand on her forehead, her strands of hair leaving traces of oil on my fingertips. "Don't go there."

"I miss her," she whispered so softly I hardly heard her. Then she opened her eyes completely, and stared into space. "I just can't get rid of this hole."

"I miss her too," I said. "Come on." I put my hand on her arm. "Let's get you up and go downstairs. I can make you tea."

She closed her eyes. "A year has passed already. A whole year without her."

"I'll make dinner," I said.

"I'll eat later," she replied.

I stared down at her. The stillness was back. I'd had her and I'd lost her.

I left the room and went downstairs and when I hit the bottom of the steps I saw that the kitchen light was on. My dad stood by the kitchen island, and was going through the mail. A package of skinless chicken breasts, and a head of cauliflower and broccoli, sat on the counter beside a white plastic grocery bag.

"Where were you, Dad?" I asked. "You were supposed to stay home with Mom!"

He placed all the mail on the counter and glanced my way. "I went and got a few groceries. I've been here all day. Your mother was up for quite a while then she said she wanted to sleep. I was only gone fifteen minutes. When did you get home?"

Since Faith died my dad did our grocery shopping and made most of our meals. "A few minutes ago," I said. "I caught the bus."

"How was *your* day?" His eyes showed his sadness, as did his voice.

I shrugged.

Two steps later he had me in his arms. I allowed myself to lean into him.

"We'll get through this," he whispered. "I wouldn't have left her if I didn't think she was okay." Then he pulled away. So I did too.

Our moment was over. Brief, but enough.

He opened the fridge and pulled out a plastic container that was filled with salad. "There's enough here for all three of us," he said. "I was going to grill some chicken to go with it." For the past three months my dad had been on a serious health kick. I often had to pick up fast food because a person can only eat so much chicken and veggies.

"Um, I'm not sure Mom is hungry."

"I'm going to try to get her to eat something."

I nodded. "You're still on your health kick, I see," I said, pointing to the chicken.

He patted his stomach. "Down forty pounds. But dying for a burger. I see your wrappers in the garbage every morning and I start drooling."

I tried to laugh at his attempt at humour. Nothing was really funny today though. "You mean a big, *juicy* burger with a delicious soft fresh bun."

He sort of smiled and pointed his finger at me. "Enough of that."

Our light moment ended and silence hovered over us, once again, until I asked, "Do you think Mom will actually eat anything?"

He blew out a rush of air. "I dunno. Lately, she's been eating oatmeal for dinner. And I'm good with that."

I forced myself to raise my eyebrows up and down. "I can make that," I said.

This time he actually laughed out loud. "You'll do fine if you go away to university next year."

University. A word I didn't want to even think about, let alone talk about. I went to the pantry and got out the oatmeal. "I'm on it," I said.

"Good boy. I'll go upstairs and talk to her."

"She might not talk back," I said.

"That's okay."

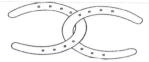

After dinner, I left the house. Sometimes in the evenings I walked for an hour just for the fresh air. Today, though, I guess I wanted to talk to someone. I yanked out my phone and called Anna.

"Hey," she said. "What are you up to?"

"Walking." I stared at the dark sky, the stars, imagining Faith as a star up there, a bright light, an angel with wings. I hoped she was flying, making friends. She'd never really had any friends. Kids didn't understand her.

"Shouldn't you be working on your English essay?" Anna asked.

And just like that I was brought back to reality. Here I was: cold, on a dark street, alone, and talking to my girlfriend when I should be doing school work. "I couldn't stay another minute in the house," I said.

"How's your mom?"

"Not too good today." Why had I called? I swiped at my eyes and kept walking. What a baby.

"Are you okay?" she asked softly.

"I'm fine." I nodded, even though I was by myself. "I made oatmeal for her and she ate some."

"Oatmeal?"

"Yeah. It's pretty much all she wants to eat these days." My teeth started chattering.

There was a silence on the other end. I could hear her breathing. Then she said, "Maybe try to get her to see someone again."

"I wish she would. My dad has tried."

"Is she taking her meds?"

"She says they make her dopey."

How I had managed to get Anna Leonard as a girlfriend is still a mystery to me. Not only does her brain work overtime, she is super

27

good-looking, half Japanese and half Caucasian, although she looks more Japanese with her long black hair. I have to admit she's the best thing that's happened to me since Faith passed away. Faith had stopped eating and my mom had done everything she could to help her. Even put her in the hospital where she was strapped down and given intravenous fluids. Then she was put in rehab and *somehow* died of organ failure. How? No one knows for sure. But she did.

"I wonder if they could change the prescription," Anna said. She has big plans to go to med school. I admire her dreams—and wish I had some of my own.

I stopped walking and stood in the middle of the sidewalk. Once again I looked upward.

Go see the horses.

Faith!

"You *are* up there," I whispered.

"Justin?" Anna's voice came through on the phone. "You still there?"

I shook my head. Man, I was losing it. "I should go," I said. "I need to get home and write my essay."

"You want to come over?" she asked.

"Nah. I'm okay."

"You sure?"

"I think I need to be alone."

"I understand."

"Later," I said.

"Later," she said softly.

I shoved my phone in my pocket and headed home. Maybe I should go see the horses with Madeline. After all, Faith had come to me and told me to.

CHAPTER THREE
MADELINE

I slid the heavy wooden door across its rollers, using all my muscles. It screeched as it rolled open. The smell of hay and horse greeted me. I inhaled. A warm sensation flowed through me and my entire body just relaxed. My brain didn't feel as if it had to work and work and work. Like it did at school. My brain has to use more brain cells than most people because of my injury, or at least that's what the doctors are always saying. In the barn, it could just be, so I could just be.

"God, it stinks in here," said Becky. "So gross."

"I liiike it," I said.

"It smells like pee!" Becky shook her head at me. "How can you like that?"

"I'm goooing to see the hooorses," I said.

I walked the length of the rickety old building. Musty windows, weathered floor, rustic wood, hanging bridles, smell of leather. Every uneven footstep made an awkward *clunk* but no one at the barn minded.

The back door was shut too and I slid it open to a blue sky with its winter sun. Willow, my favourite horse, was outside, basking in the afternoon warmth. As soon as she saw me, she clip-clopped over. Becky had her head buried in her phone and I quickly shut the door so Willow didn't go into the barn and try to escape out the front door. Sometimes she was naughty and liked to run away to find grass to eat. I carefully stepped down the wooden ramp, working on my balance. Willow was at the bottom, waiting for me.

From my pocket I pulled out some carrots, leftover from my lunch. I held out my hand. Her lips quivered and flapped as she took the carrot, gobbling it down. Willow only came up to my waist and to me she was the prettiest miniature at the barn. I even wrote a poem about her.

Half black, half white.
Polka dots scattered like paint drops.
Black legs with white ankle socks.
A mix, more than one colour,
a little body with artistic designs.
Horses can be tall or tiny,
thick or trim.
Black, or white,
or
brown with white spots,
white spots with black.
All beautiful. Like humans.

I recited the poem in my head. I had written it for English class and got an A: my best mark ever. Math sucks. Reading is hard. Writing is hard too but if I take my time I can do it because I can pick away at the computer keys at my own pace. I suck at cursive writing, big time. My brain just doesn't get the signals to my hand properly or fast enough.

Willow *is* a mix, just like the description in my poem. The front half of her body is all black and her back half has black and white spots, like polka dots. Her legs are all black but just above her hooves she has a little spattering of white. And she has a pretty white stripe down her nose too. I'd forgotten to put that in the poem.

"Goood giiirl," I said.

I ran my hand up and down her nose, scratching her a little because that is what she likes best. She whinnied and I bent over and kissed her on the nose.

"Hi, you," said Tonya.

"Hiii, Tooonya."

Tonya Simmons owns the four miniature horses that she uses for therapy for kids. I had started coming to see the horses for therapy, a year after my accident. Now I am considered a volunteer.

"You just get here?" Tonya asked. Tonya's black afro bobbed in the sunlight, and her eyes danced like always.

I nodded. "I'll cleeean the staaalls," I said.

Tonya stroked Willow and cooed at her. Happy with the attention, Willow whinnied back.

"Priiinceeess," I said, laughing.

"She is, at that."

I heard the barn door open and looked over. Becky stood there with her arms crossed, looking miserable. "Weee neeeed to cleeean the staaalls," I said.

Becky moaned. "I don't want to do Cher and Daphne's."

Cher and Daphne shared a stall because Cher was the mom and Daphne was the baby. Cher was still nursing Daphne.

Tonya grinned. "I guess you don't like dealing with two poops for the price of one?"

"No. I don't."

"I'll dooo iiit," I said.

Tonya shrugged. "Okay. Becky, you clean Cowboy's then. When you're finished, Madeline, meet me outside by the riding ring. We have some new little ones coming in and I'll need you to walk the horses around."

I held up my thumb and smiled.

Tonya left and I went back into the barn. The instructions for what

31

I needed to do were written on the barn bulletin board. I went over and read them. Like my locker combination, I needed help remembering so Tonya had me write the instructions down.

Once I had the instructions in my head, I got a shovel and headed to Cher and Daphne's stall. Becky leaned up against a wooden post and watched me.

"I didn't think the two-for-one poop comment was even funny," she said.

I laughed. "I diiid."

"Whatever." Becky stomped over to Cowboy's stall. Cowboy was our male.

The work of cleaning the stall used my muscles. My body was too uncoordinated to do many sports anymore. Before my accident I'd played soccer and took ballet lessons and did gymnastics. Now, I swam a bit but it seemed everything I did was for rehab. So boring. I kept thinking that if I could get my brain to work, maybe I could try real horseback riding. That was what I really wanted to do but my mother thought I would fall off. The height scared her. I shovelled the poop into the middle of the stall, so I could gather it all before I put it in the wheelbarrow.

Once the wheelbarrow was full, I swept the floor. And then came my favourite part, sprinkling the deodorizer and putting fresh chips down. The chips have a sweet smell to them, almost lavender-like. When I was done I headed over to help Becky. When I got to Cowboy's stall, she was on her phone and hadn't even started her cleaning yet.

"Cool, see ya in a few," she said. She glanced at me out of the corner of her eye then whispered, "I gotta go."

"Is thaaat Mooolly?"

"Yeah," said Becky. She avoided looking at me and picked up her shovel.

"I'll heeelp you," I said. "We caaan put hiiis poop iiin myyy wheelbaaarrow."

"Thanks." She glanced at the door of the barn.

Side by side we worked, not talking, but like when we were little, we instinctively knew who would do what. Becky was finishing up the shovelling, so I went to get the deodorizer. Through the sweet smell of the clean stalls, I smelled the cigarette smoke. I glanced up to see Molly and Cassandra. What were *they* doing here?

"Yoooou caaan't...smoke in heeere." I spoke loudly because no one should smoke in a barn; that was a complete no-no. What if a spark landed on the hay? And people thought I was stupid.

"Come on," said Becky, jerking her head to the door. "Maddie's right. Let's blow out of here."

"Yoooou're leeeaving?" I stared at Becky.

She came over to me, put her hand on my shoulder, and said, "Come on, Maddie. You like the horses. I don't. When Mom comes, tell her I went to a friend's house to study. Or better yet, tell her I brought you here but I had soooo much work to do I had to leave."

Cassandra and Molly laughed. "Study? Yeah, right."

"Yoooou want meee to liiie?" I asked Becky.

"It's not really a lie." Becky grinned at her friends before she turned back to me. "We're going to study...fermentation."

This made Cassandra and Molly burst into hysterics.

"Good one," said Molly. "Or how about liquidation?"

"Combined with smoke inhalation," said Cassandra.

Becky held up her pinky finger. "Besties," she said to me in her sugar-coated voice. I knew she didn't mean it. First time ever. Our pinky shake was *our* thing and we'd done it since before my accident.

I shook my head.

"I'll dump the wheelbarrow first," she said, still holding up her finger.

"Dooon't booother." I marched over to the wheelbarrow and picked it up. I left the barn, going out the back door, ignoring Becky and her friends laughing as they left out the front door.

After I'd dumped the contents of the wheelbarrow into the pile of manure, which got made into some type of compost, I headed to the ring where Tonya was putting little padded saddles on the horses. When I say little, I mean little. They were made of cushioned cloth, not leather, and they tied up under the horse's belly. Willow's was purple.

Once the padding was on, Tonya placed a little girl named Samira on Willow. The outdoor ring was fairly big and we walked along the wooden fence. Tonya held Samira up on Willow and I held onto the lead. Samira is three and has something called Angelman syndrome and because of that she smiles and laughs a lot, which I like because it makes me think she is always enjoying Willow. Plus, she is teeny-tiny small. To me, it seems as if Willow smiles when she walks, like she knows she's doing something really good for someone.

Snow crunched under my feet and a refreshing, cold wind nipped at my cheeks. Willow performed perfectly.

After three times around we stopped, and Tonya lifted Samira off and allowed her to pet Willow. Willow nuzzled her head into Samira and she giggled. Willow is such a show-off.

Samira's father came over to get her and when they were gone, Tonya said, "Thanks, Madeline."

"Haaaappy to heeelp," I said.

"I'm sorry Becky left," she said.

I shrugged and looked at my toes. "She haaad to stuudy."

"Do you want to clean Willow's hooves?"

I nodded. "I'll bruuush heeer too."

I went back to the barn and got the box that was labelled *Willow*. There was a bigger brush for her mane and a littler brush that had a pick on the end to clean her hooves. Thrush infections are common with horses, especially if the hooves aren't cleaned. As I was brushing Willow, Daphne came over and nudged me. "Okaaay," I laughed. "I'll giiive you a caaarrot."

Daphne is only a year old and super friendly but she's a bit of a brat. Or at least that's what Tonya says about her, but in a good way.

The job of cleaning the hooves always takes more time. I had just finished Willow's hooves when I heard the car engine and the sound of tires on the dirt road. I looked up and saw my mom's car just as it bumped through a big rut. I had been dreading her arrival since Becky left.

"There's your mom," said Tonya. "Are you coming on Saturday?"

I nodded. I thought about Justin and how I had asked him to come. "Caaan I briiing a frieeend?"

"What kind of friend?" She narrowed her eyes a little.

I wondered if she asked that because of Becky's friends. "Myyy Best Buuuddy at schoooool."

"Oh, that's supposed to be a good program. Okay, sure. I would like him to fill out a volunteer form and a waiver, if that's okay. I can email it to you."

"I will priiint it fooor him," I said.

"I'm always game for more volunteers, as long as he follows the rules, like you do. I think you might be one of my best volunteers."

"Heee wiiill," I said, smiling.

"Say goodbye to Willow," she said, patting Willow on the neck. "She's gonna miss you. She always does."

I kissed Willow's nose and scratched it one last time. "You beee a good giiirl," I said. "I'll beee baaack on Saaaturdaaay aaand I'll briiing you sooome aaapples."

Willow whinnied and blinked and that meant she liked the idea of my bringing her apples. She understood me. Every word.

I could see my mother walking toward the ring, a big smile on her face, and I knew I had to go. I also knew that smile was soon going to disappear.

"Hi, Madeline." She touched my shoulder. "How was your day, honey?"

"Gooood," I said.

"Where's Becky?" She scanned the yard behind me.

"Stuuudying," I replied, lowering my head. Maybe I wasn't really lying. Okay, I was.

"Where?"

"Wiiith frieeends."

"She *left*?"

I stared at my boot, not able to meet my mother's gaze.

"What friends is she with?" My mom's tone was sharp.

I shrugged.

She blew out air before she clamped her lips together in one tight line. "Oh, that girl," she muttered.

Then she asked, "Did she say when she was coming home?"

I shook my head.

Mom put her hand on my back and sighed. "I'm sorry," she said. "This isn't your fault. Go get your backpack. We'll go home."

I went back in the barn, put Willow's brushes away, and filled out the chart to say what I had done. Then I slowly headed outside to the car.

When I got in the car, my mother eyed me. "Do you really have no idea where she went?"

"I...I tooold you. Sheee's with frieeends."

"That's all you know about this? You usually know everything."

I shook my head. "Nooot anymooore."

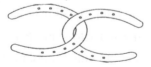

Becky didn't show up for dinner and my mom kept checking her phone for a text message. None.

"Maaaybe she weeent to Daaad's." I carried my dinner dishes to the sink. "Teeext hiiim." My mom and dad were divorced so he lived at a different house.

She waved her hand in front of her face. "He's on a business trip."

I rinsed my plate and put it in the dishwasher.

"Do you have homework?" she asked.

"Sooome."

"When you're done, why don't we practise what you learned in speech therapy this week?"

I closed my eyes for a second. My dreaded speech therapy.

"You must have learned something new," said my mother.

I hadn't learned anything new because I still couldn't do the old stuff. In normal people the brain is like this boss who sends millions of impulses (big therapy word) to muscles. Mine is so trashed that it doesn't send those millions out. Or if it does, it sends them the wrong way. I'm supposed to practise so many things every day to try and get the wires reconnected to go the right way.

When I didn't answer she said, "Remember, practice helps."

I turned to face her. "Yooou thiiink I don't knooow *thaaat*?"

"I know it's hard. But you have to practise to get better. It's like anything in life. I'm here to help you practise, to make it easier."

"It iiis haaard. Reeeally haaard."

"Don't you want to get better?"

"Whyyy would yooou even aaask thaaat?" My body started to shake. My hands trembled. My heart raced. *Oh no.* "Of couuurse I dooo!" I yelled. I actually wanted to slam something but I didn't. I stood still, rigid.

Mom stood and walked over to me and gave me a hug. "Madeline, I know it's hard, honey. But it's so important that you keep working."

Her hug helped relax my body a little. She *was* right. "I know," I whispered.

She pulled back and lifted my chin with her finger. "I'm only pushing you because I love you."

I nodded just as the back door slammed. My mom let go of me and walked briskly to the mud room.

Becky's timing was perfect. Now, maybe, I could get out of doing my speech stuff with Mom and could do it in my room, by myself. My mom nagged too much.

I heard Becky's voice. "Hi, Mom."

"Where have you been? I've been worried sick."

"Studying. Didn't Maddie tell you?"

"I would like you to answer my text messages."

"My phone died."

I shook my head. Her phone didn't die. Even I knew that.

"You smell like smoke," said my mother.

"Not my fault. Molly's father smokes. *Pee-yoo*."

I giggled to hear Becky say *pee-yoo* and I knew she was making my mother's head spin right about now.

"Nice try, Becky," said my mom. "I can smell it on your breath."

"What's for dinner?" Becky walked into the kitchen and she had this smirk on her face. My mother trailed her, shaking her head.

"Diiid you stuuudy looots?" I asked.

Becky winked at me and mouthed *thanks* before she said, "Oh yeah. Tons."

Then she walked over to the oven and lifted the lid on the crock pot. "Yum," she said. "Pea soup."

"Yooou haate pea soooup," I said.

"Oh right," she said. "I do hate pea soup."

"Becky, I'd like you to tell me more about these girls you were with," said my mother.

"You know them," she said. "Sarah and Amy."

Okay. Another lie. That was my cue to leave. "I'm goooing to myyy rooooom," I said.

Up in my room I practised phrases that had tons of vowels. I was supposed to say them over and over. And try to say them faster each time. When my words started tumbling, I slowed down again. The thing was I always slowed at the same spot, or so it seemed to me.

I was midway through a sentence when I heard the knock on my door. Crap. It was probably my mother. Before I could say anything the door pushed open a little and I saw Becky peeking in my room.

"You need help?" she asked.

"Suuure," I said. If my mom saw Becky helping, she would leave me alone.

Becky came in and sat beside me on my bed.

"Whyyy dooo yoooou liiike smooooking?" I asked.

She shrugged. "I don't really like it. It makes me so dizzy."

"Theeen don't dooo iiit."

She tapped the phrase I had been working on. "Say it," she said.

"Whyyy are yoooou haaanging with thooose giiirls?"

"Those aren't the words I'm reading," she said.

"I waaanna know whyyy."

She frowned at me. "Why do you have to bug me too? It's enough that Mom is on my case, like twenty-four-seven I might add. I like them because they make me forget."

"Foorget whaat?"

She jumped off my bed. "I wanted to help you but you *clearly* don't want my help. I don't need a second Mom." She stomped out of my room.

I lay on my bed and stared at the ceiling. Forget?

Was it *me* she wanted to forget?

CHAPTER FOUR
JUSTIN

A big red 62% stared at me from the top corner of my English essay. I threw it in my backpack. That mark wasn't getting me into university. Why did I even think I had to go to university?

Because it was all everyone talked about in senior year.

With my head down I left the classroom. Anna was waiting for me and a part of me didn't want to see her. School and grades and tests were her life.

"How'd you do?" she asked.

"Okay," I lied.

"I can't believe she only gave me an 88%," she moaned. "I spent so much time on it. I don't know how she marks. I can't figure her out. Even my bibliography was perfect."

"You coming to the gym at lunch?" I asked, quickly changing the subject. We were having a Best Buddies game time at lunch, something new and different. If it was a success I wanted to see if it could replace our regular meeting although…we had a few with extreme OCD in the group and they didn't like change.

"Of course." She linked her arm in mine. "Should be fun."

We walked a few strides before she said, "Oh, I forgot to tell you. I got another early acceptance. From McGill. My mom thinks it's a great school but I'm still set on going to Stanford though. They have such a good science program."

"What happened to the University in Los Angeles?"

"I decided against it," she said.

"Stanford is still California," I said. "Congrats on McGill though."

"You'll visit if I go to California?" She squeezed my hand. "And I'll visit you in your dorm."

A knot seemed to appear in my chest, making it constrict. Dorm. University. I glanced at Anna as we continued to walk down the hall. Were we delusional in thinking we could do that long distance thing after high school?

She squeezed my hand and I knew she was waiting for an answer. "Sure," I said, just to say something.

"Tell me you've put out a few applications..."

"Not yet," I mumbled.

She stopped walking and turned me to face her. "Are you going to?"

"I'm not sure." My grades had been so crappy lately. And then there was my mother. How could I leave her and leave my dad to deal with our family alone?

"I can help you," she said. "If you want to bring up your marks."

I pulled away from Anna. "I'm just not sure I want to go to school next year. Well, university."

"Okay," she said, but it wasn't as if it was an *okay* like she agreed—it was an *okay* with a question mark.

I started walking again. "I don't even know what I want to major in."

She linked her arm into mine and pressed her cheek against my upper arm. "You don't have to decide that right away." Suddenly, she lifted her head. "What about something like social work? Or—"

"Let's not talk about this now."

"Okay," she said. This time there was no lingering question mark. "How's Madeline?"

"Great," I said, thankful for the change of topic. "She wants me to go see the miniature horses with her. I guess they're used for therapy."

"That's like social work. Why don't you look at social work?"

"Look, can we just drop it?" I snapped.

She stepped away from me and put up her hands. I could see the tears welling in her eyes. "Sorry that I care about you." Then she turned and took off at a rapid clip, her head held high and shoulders square.

What was wrong with me? I shouldn't have barked at her. I watched her go, not able to open my mouth and call to her, tell her to wait, tell her I was sorry.

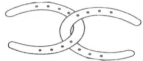

My black mood hadn't lifted by lunch but I made my way to the gymnasium, hoping to appear happier than I was. I had to. I was the Chapter President and it was my job. With every step I took, my mood lightened a little in anticipation of a game of dodgeball. Easy dodgeball. Like, dodgeball where the ball had to roll on the ground. And how much fun everyone was still going to have with that.

Still, Anna had made me think. I wondered about social workers and if they had moments where someone had a breakthrough and where they felt great that they had done something for someone. I needed to apologize to her. Seriously. I was the one in the wrong.

When I rounded the corner to the secondary gym, which was smaller than the big gym, I saw Becky standing with Madeline by the doors.

Just seeing Madeline's smiling face lifted my mood. "Hiya, Madeline," I said.

"What? No hello for me?" said Becky in this forced, sugary tone. Something was up.

I shook my head at her. "You didn't give me a chance. Hi. Becky."

"You could say it nicer than that." She gave me a flirty smile. "But that's okay."

"What's with you?" I frowned at her.

"Well, I was thinking that you…" She put her finger on my chest and traced it down to my navel. It took all my energy not to swat it away, but I didn't want to do that in front of Madeline. But I did take a step back.

"Just spit it out." I didn't have a lot of time and patience for this kind of girl.

"That you," she said coyly, "should go with Madeline to see the horses that she loves so much. On Saturday. I convinced my mother it would be a good thing."

Ignoring Becky, I turned to Madeline. "Madeline, I would like to see the horses, but not because Becky wants me to but because you asked me. What time on Saturday?"

Her eyes lit up and her smile spread across her entire face. It was so infectious that I smiled back, first one of the day. I was so glad I had decided to do this. "Teeeen," she said.

I held up my thumb. "I'll be there."

Becky touched my cheek. "You are honestly the best Best Buddy my sis could have."

I shook my head to get her finger off my face. "I'm not sure what you *really* want but I bet it's not good."

Then I heard the voice. "What's going on here?" Anna. Oh man. This wasn't the way I wanted to apologize.

"Nothing," said Becky giggling.

Anna slipped her arm firmly in mine. Fortunately, others from our Best Buddies group, including Harrison (Anna's buddy), starting showing up, and she moved away to talk to him. And Becky's phone pinged, telling her she had a text from someone way more important than me, so she high-tailed it down the hall.

"Time to go in the gym," I said to Madeline. "You can help me get the balls out."

Once we were in the gym, and I had the dodgeballs unlocked I gathered everyone in the middle. "Okay," I said in front of the group. "There are a few rules."

Everyone listened as I went over how Best Buddies would work as teams. And how you couldn't aim for anyone's head. And the key wasn't to hit the person hard but to run to stay away from getting hit. Once caught, you were to get a ball from the bin and try to get the others. And when there was one group left they were the winners but it wasn't about winning it was about having fun. Big spiel. I actually practised it last night.

I motioned for Madeline to join me at the front, so that we could demonstrate being the "it" couple.

I leaned in to her and said, "You're going to yell, *Ready, Set, Go*. Okay?"

"Meee?" she said, looking up at me. "Buuut I taaalk slooow."

"No one will mind," I said.

"Reeeady. Seeet. Gooo!" she bellowed.

Everyone started running and shrieking, of course. At first Erika, (who was born with Down syndrome), held her hands over her ears because of her sensitive hearing but then Gianni (her Best Buddy) took her hand and they started running, around and around. Harrison, with his high-functioning autism, usually didn't like this kind of game, so he stood still at first, but then Anna talked to him and he actually started running with her—clumsily, but he was moving. I cracked a smile.

Gloria was the screamer and Willa did her best to keep up with her, but in her skater shoes that weren't even laced up, it wasn't as easy as it looked. Dan, who was also born with Down syndrome, like Erika, ran around and around and around because he loved anything to do with sports: You name it, he did it. In fact, he was training for the Special Olympics in basketball. His Best Buddy, Marcie, was on the senior basketball team and also played in city leagues, so she easily ran with him.

A few of the others walked, like Stuart, (Stuart also has FAS), and his buddy Sam, who was terrific with him because he loved to tell jokes and make him laugh.

I gave Madeline the ball and whispered. "Mohammad is open. Throw it at him." Mohammad was walking with his Best Buddy, Ciara. She has Williams syndrome and was dancing instead of running.

Madeline tried, but she's a little uncoordinated so the ball went sideways. I ran and picked up the ball and brought it back to her. "Let's try again."

This time I helped her and the ball trickled over to Willa who made a show of getting caught, by throwing her arms in the air. "You got me!" She pretended to fall to the ground because that's who Willa was. Gloria ran over to her and tried to pull her up and I gently threw the ball so it hit Gloria.

Then Willa said, "Come on Gloria, let's get a ball!"

We managed to fit in two games. Dan and Marcie won both because no one could catch Dan who did lap after lap. Since this was something the Best Buddies had never tried before, I was happy with the success.

"Come on in, everyone." Ten minutes remained in the lunch period.

Once I had the group gathered in front of me, I asked, "Does anyone want to do this again?"

"Yeah!" Big cheers.

"I like it better than meetings," said Dan. He was still panting from running. "I l-liked running." He spit his words out before he thumped on his chest. "No one c-could c-catch me."

"Me too," said Gloria. "I liked 'getting' people though. We hit Justin." She put her hand over her mouth and laughed.

"We sure did," said Willa. She patted Gloria on the back.

"I agree," I said. "It's so much better to be active."

Sam patted Stuart on the back. "We were awesome."

Stuart held up his hand to show four fingers. "Four, we got four." He sang his words and put his hand under his leg to show his four fingers, making huge gestures. Then he put his fingers behind his head and wiggled them. Stuart laughed and then we all laughed.

Even me.

After the giggles started to die down, I held up my hands. "Okay, okay, listen up, everyone. This might be as good a time as any to talk about our next event. Go ahead, Marcie."

"I have a friend at St. Francis High School," said Marcie. "She's also in their Best Buddies program and they have an Evening of Friendship coming up and they thought it might be fun to invite us. They're holding the event at their local neighbourhood community centre."

"That sounds like fun," said Mohammed.

"I'd be game for that," said Willa. "Can you get more info?"

"Sure," said Marcie. "It would be just our two schools. We'd have to get permission from the parents to go to another venue. I think, but don't quote me, that they're having music and food."

"Maybe we can play games with them," said Dan.

"Good thought," said Marcie. "I can talk to my friend about that."

"We could also help with food," said Anna.

"We could do hip hop," said Erika. She did one of her funky moves.

"Hey, what about one of those photo booths," said Stuart. "I was at a wedding and they had one of those and it was a blast."

"Great idea," I said. "I'll check with the other school and see if between the two of us we can budget this in."

"Do we need to organize rides?" Willa asked.

"Parents would probably have to drive," said Anna.

"I'm sure my mother would drive," said Harrison. "Although, she only has five seatbelts and it is a law, so we could only be able to take four passengers and I would be included in that four so only three others could travel safely with us."

"Thank you, Harrison," I said. "We'll talk to your mother."

I glanced at the clock. "Lunch is almost over. Since there are details to hash over we will need a few volunteers to make it work. But let's call it a day for today."

When the meeting ended, I walked over to Madeline, who was with Willa and Gloria. "Do you want me to walk you to class?" I asked her. "I just have to lock up the balls."

"I'll walk with her," said Willa, putting her hand on Madeline's shoulder. "We're in the same class. This girl writes some mean poetry."

"I'll teeext Mr. Siiingh. Heee caaan meet meee theeere."

"You never told me you liked to write," I said.

She just shrugged. "Eeeasier thaaan taaalking." Then she rolled her eyes. "Aaand maaath."

"Math's not my favourite either. Hey, I'd love to read some of your writing, if you like to show your work."

"I wrooote one abooout the Beeest Buuuddies," she said, lowering her head shyly.

"Wow. Really? We should read it at a meeting."

By the shrug of her shoulders, and the smile on her face, I figured she wouldn't mind that. Suddenly, the five-minute warning bell interrupted us. "You better go," I said. "See you Saturday."

"Yooou'll looove the hooorses," she said.

"I'm sure I will."

They walked away and I wheeled the ball cart to the storage room. Thinking I was alone, I started whistling.

"You're happy." I heard Anna's voice.

I glanced at her as she walked toward me, then I pulled the door shut on the storage room and tested it to see if it was locked.

"Hey, listen," I said turning around to face her, but not really meeting her eyes. "I'm sorry about earlier."

"I'm sorry too," she said. "I get excited for school and I know not everyone does. But then, talking about school makes me think of us being apart. My emotions are all over the place."

I reached for her and we hugged. Then I kissed her, knowing no one was around.

CHAPTER FIVE
MADELINE

Becky yanked out a pink long-sleeved t-shirt from her closet. She pulled the shirt off the hanger and flung it on the bed. "You want this?"

I was in her room, sitting on the bed, watching her go through her closet. We'd just got home from school. Green, yellow, and pink shirts were heaped on her bed.

"I liiike piiink," I said. And I did. I picked up the shirt. "It's soooft."

"We have to trade," she said. "That's a good silk shirt. I've only worn it once. I want your black one from Urban Outfitters."

Black one? I couldn't think fast enough.

"You know. The one with the buttons on the sleeve."

"Uh. Okaaay." I still couldn't bring the shirt up in my mind. I closed my eyes. *Think. Think. Stupid brain, think.* I squeezed my eyes. I kept thinking.

"It also has a v-neck," said Becky.

Then… I saw it. I opened my eyes and picked up the pink shirt. "I'll traaade," I said.

"Great," said Becky. She pulled out a deep purple shirt. "Hmmm. I kind of like this one." She held it up to her torso and was looking at herself in the mirror. "Yup, it's a keeper." She put it back then pulled out a red shirt.

"This one is like *blood*," she said. "It's a huge keeper."

A memory surfaced in my brain of Becky and me, and we were riding our bikes but this time she fell, not me, and skinned her leg and cried because there was blood. "You haaate blood," I said. Funny thing is,

I can remember lots of things from before my accident. It's recent things that I struggle with.

"Not anymore." She pushed all the shirts she didn't want off the bed and sat beside me. "You can have any of those if you give me all your black ones."

"Diiid I bleeeed when I feeell?"

"Not sure," said Becky quickly.

"I wiiish I could reeemembeeer."

Becky shook her head. "No, you don't. Let's talk about something else. Like black shirts."

"I dooon't have maaany black ooones," I said. Becky always changed the topic when I asked her about my fall.

"Oh, right, because Mom's got you dressing like you're five again."

"Nooo, sheee doooesn't."

"Yes. She. Does. She shouldn't treat you like you're still eight. It's like you just stopped at that age. We're fourteen, almost fifteen." She pulled her knees up and circled her arms around them. "And she shouldn't treat me like such a baby either."

"I dooon't waaant to dreeess like yooou. All blaaack."

"What's wrong with black? Your *stupid* Best Buddy wears black." She curled up the side of her lip and rolled her eyes.

"Heee's not stuuupid."

"Okay, whatever. He might not be stupid but he is soooooo boring." She flopped back on her bed.

"Heee's nooot," I said. I didn't like it when she talked about Justin like that. Anyway, today she had been touching him like she liked him. "You...liiiked him toooday," I said.

"No, I didn't. I just wanted him to do something for me." She sat up. "Maddie, he has to go to the horses with you on Saturday. It's important."

"He saaaid he waaas." I had heard him say that he would and so had

Becky. Why was she saying he wouldn't come? He said he would. I could feel my body getting hot, and my head started pounding. I tried to breathe and relax the muscles in my face.

"Good," said Becky. "'Cause I don't want to go. If he goes then maybe I don't have to, and if Mom drives you then I can stay home by myself. He better go."

"He saaaid he wooould!" I yelled. My words just blurted out. I hate when this happens. *Hate it. Hate it. Hate it.* Becky immediately turned to me.

"Maddie, it's okay." She put her arm around me. Her touch, for some reason, made me think of how she had talked to Justin today and how she had touched him. It wasn't right. And I didn't like that she had done that. My head was spinning.

"Dooon't touch meee!" I screeched so loud it hurt the back of my throat.

"Maddie, I said it's okay. I'm sorry."

"Heee's not boooring!"

Suddenly, my mom burst into Becky's room. "What is going on in here?"

Becky stood up. "Maddie's freaking out. For no reason."

"She must have a reason," said my mom. "Are you provoking her?"

"Oh, come on. You know that sometimes she freaks for *absolutely* no reason, Mom. She can't help it."

My mom turned to me. "Are you okay?" she asked gently.

I lowered my head and stared at the carpet. Again, I breathed, in and out, and tried to relax my body. Seconds later I was not so worked up. "Yeees," I replied.

I heard my mother sigh before she said, "You need to practise your piano before your lesson, Becky. You have an exam coming up." She was talking to Becky because I didn't play piano anymore.

Becky moaned. "I told you, I want to quit. Maddie got to quit."

At the mention of my name, I lifted my head. My mom crossed her arms in front of her chest and just stared at Becky. "And you know how hard it was for her."

Here we go again, I thought. Another fight. This time about piano. I hadn't wanted to quit piano, (Becky and I started lessons when we were five), but it had been so frustrating when I couldn't remember the notes. I would pound the keys and throw hissy fits and Mom said it would be better for me to try some other form of art. She'd put me in painting classes and bead-making classes and pottery classes. Secretly, I started writing poetry. I like doing it best because I can go at my own speed and I don't have to take a class with other people. In classes I'm always "the brain-damaged one."

"It's hard for me too," snapped Becky, "with stupid schoolwork piling up. I hate piano. And I hate those dumb *advanced* classes."

"You have such talent," said my mother. "Don't throw it away."

"I didn't ask to be talented in *piano.*"

I sat on the bed, with my head lowered and tried not to listen to the back-and-forth between them.

"You can finish out the year and we'll talk about this in the summer."

"I want to quit now!" Becky screamed at Mom.

"Becky, this discussion is over. Now, you need to go downstairs and practise."

"No!"

The sound of Becky's yelling hit the inside of my skull. A rush of anger circled my head. I wished I could play piano. My head ached. She could play and didn't want to. I couldn't stand the pounding against my skull. It hurt. It hurt. It hurt.

So I started hitting my head with my hand, over and over. More hurt. More hurt.

My mother tried to take hold of my hand but I just kept hitting.

Becky kneeled down in front of me. "Maddie, I'm here," she said softly. She gently took my hand and as quickly as the fit came, it left. Becky wrapped her arms around me and I rested my head on her shoulder. Fits always made me so tired.

"Maybe we should take you to your room," said my mom.

My mom reached out to take my hand but I shook my head. "I'm nooot a baaaby. I huuurt my heeead." I had been taught in therapy to tell people when I could do something but to also know when to ask for help.

"You're right," said my mother.

I got up to leave and Becky handed me the pink shirt. "It's yours. I don't need to trade. It'll look good on you."

"Thaaanks," I said.

Once in my room, I lay on my bed, curled into a ball and stared at the wall. Mom was right. I had to keep working to get better, get my wires working again. But sometimes the work was so hard. I closed my eyes and saw myself riding my bike with Becky. We loved racing against each other, our streamers flying in the wind.

I sat up, took my computer off my nightstand, and fired it up.

I started writing. Fingers pressing letters. Slowly. One word. One line. Then another.

My mother peeked in my door, and I told her I was fine. I wanted to be alone. She said okay.

A good hour later I had this:

Bubble gum pink bikes.
Helmets, crayon yellow and sky blue,
with streaks of neon pink.
Birthday gifts,
complete with silver bells and white baskets.
Two of them. Identical.

Streamers flying in the wind.
Wind blowing in long hair.
I win. Cross the line first. Over and over.
Until…
Crash, smack, boom, whatever.
That day. What happened?

I read the poem over and knew it needed work. What else could I put in it? How could I change it? Maybe too many colours? I leaned my head back. Birthdays had always been a big deal back then, with cake and presents and a party, always a party with loot bags. Now I didn't have birthday parties. Forget about that.

Before my accident, I had always beaten Becky at everything. I could stay underwater longer, run faster, bike harder, but then I fell. I remember my dad always saying I was his little athlete. My parents were still together on the day of my accident. After was when it all went downhill. We had been out front of our house and my dad had his back turned, watering the flowers. My mom blamed him for not watching us.

I glanced at my poem and following the line "*That day. What happened?*" I typed in the word "*Blame.*"

I heard a knock on my door and quickly shut my computer. "Maddie, can I come in? Maybe stay with you until dinner?"

"Yeeaah," I answered.

Becky opened my door and came over to my bed. She lay down beside me, snuggling in so she could wrap her arms around me. Then she put her pinky finger up in front of me. "Besties," she said.

I hooked my finger in hers. "Beeesties," I said.

She put her head on my back and we breathed as if we were one.

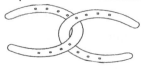

After finishing my homework, I went into the living room where the piano was sitting, polished and gleaming as always. My mom used to be a piano teacher before she and my father split and she'd had to go back to work full time at a bank. I knew she was in the shower so it was a good time to play without her coming in and trying to help me.

I sat down and stared at the black and white keys. Why couldn't I remember some of the songs I'd played before my accident? I'd had lessons and even taken my grade-one exam. The only thing I could play now was *Twinkle Twinkle Little Star* and *Mary Had a Little Lamb* and that's because Becky had recently taught them to me. But even those songs were hard on my brain. Piano was like math. It was like my brain couldn't get the info to my fingers. I also had problems with the pedals. My brain wouldn't help my feet.

I made my way through my two-song repertoire, playing the songs three times each. I heard feet on the floor and was about to shut the cover to hide the keys when Becky came in the room.

"I'll teach you another one," she said. "*Heart and Soul.* We can play it as a duet."

She sat down beside me on the piano bench and showed me my part in the duet. I sort of learned it, and Becky was patient. My mother tried to be patient, but she always ended up nagging. Within fifteen minutes, we could sort of play the song, because my part was fairly easy. All was good until my mom came in the room.

"That's great," she said. "I'm impressed."

"Beeecky is a gooood teeeacher," I said.

"I know," said my mother. "And she can play well too, if she puts her mind to it."

Becky slammed the keys. Then she stood up. "Would you get off my case for once? I practised for 45 minutes."

"I was trying to give you a compliment," said my mother.

Sometimes I felt sorry for Becky and sometimes I felt sorry for my mom. This time, I felt sorry for both of them. They could talk, *say* the words right, but they still couldn't *get* the right words.

"Yeah, right," snapped Becky. "That was a dig and you know it." She stormed out of the room.

My mother came over to the piano bench. "I can play that song with you," she said. "It's good for your memory."

"Stooop fiiighting with Beeecky," I said.

She sighed. "Agreed."

"I'll plaaay if yooou dooon't try and teeeach. Juuust let meee plaaay."

"Deal," she said, holding up her hand.

I gently hit her hand. Then we played the song, and both of us allowed the piano to speak.

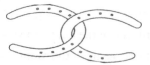

The truce lasted between Mom and Becky until Saturday morning. When my mom knocked on my door at 8:30, I was already dressed. I'd read through my daily instructions in my phone, and I checked my notebook where I keep other reminders. Today was barn day so I needed to wear barn clothes.

"It's time to get up," she said, pushing open my door.

"I'm uuup," I said.

"Did you remember to wear tights under your jeans?"

"Yeees."

"Don't forget to tie your hair back."

I picked up my phone and notebook from beside my bed and waved them at her. "Iii knooow."

"I just thought I'd check," she said.

"Iii'm fiiine."

She sighed and shut my door. I finished getting dressed then went to the kitchen.

"I don't want to go to the barn," said Becky.

"You should go with Madeline. You girls don't do much together anymore. This is a special time."

"She doesn't need me," she said. "Anyway, that Best Buddy guy is going to be there. He can help her."

I sat down at my seat at the kitchen table. "I caaan go byyy myseeelf," I said.

My mother walked over to me and placed a bowl of oatmeal in front of me. "Of course you can. But this is a nice thing that the two of you can do as sisters."

"Oh my god," said Becky. "Why can't she have her thing and I have mine?" Becky made big gestures with her hands.

"Because your thing is trouble and that doesn't cut it as a *thing*." My mother poured herself a cup of coffee. "Anyway, your dad is picking you up from the barn. I just got off the phone with him. He got in earlier than expected and does want to see you this weekend."

"Dad's picking us up?" Becky's demeanor changed and she was suddenly happier.

My mother narrowed her eyes at her. "Why the change in mood?"

Becky shrugged. "I dunno. We can have Chinese food tonight."

My mother exhaled loudly. Then under her breath but loud enough for us to hear she said, "It better not have MSG in it."

The ride over was quiet, except for Becky singing in the front seat to the music on the radio. We got to the barn early and Becky and I got out of the car, taking our overnight bags with us. I had clothes at my dad's but there were a few other things I wanted to take. Becky's bag was bulging. We walked toward the barn and Becky kept turning to see where Mom was. As soon as her car was out of sight she said, "You go in. I've got a call to make."

Today, I had brought apple chunks. I walked the length of the barn and headed outside and down the ramp. All the horses were already outside. As I was feeding Willow, I heard footsteps coming down the ramp and I turned around.

"Yooou caaame!"

"Of course," Justin replied, smiling at me.

"Meeeet Wiiillow," I said.

"I've never really seen one of these little horses up close." He approached Willow and scratched her nose. She whinnied in delight and Justin laughed. "She sure likes that," he said.

"Kiiisses too," I said. I kissed her nose and she blinked at me.

"I haven't been near a horse in a long time." Justin kneeled down and patted Willow's back. "She's beautiful," he said. "My sister would have loved this little girl."

"Diiid she riiide biiig hooorses?" One day I wanted to ride a big horse.

"She did," he said. "But I know she would have loved these little ones. She loved doing everything, even cleaning up the manure. She could spend hours at the barn."

"Meee too," I said., "I'm... soooorry she diiied."

For a moment he looked sad but then he cracked a smile and stroked Willow's neck again.

"Thanks, Madeline. For inviting me here." He looked at me. "Did you know that the branches of a willow tree bend but don't often break? I love her name."

CHAPTER SIX
JUSTIN

The alarm on my phone went off at nine and I got up right away. I didn't have a lot of time since I had to catch a bus then walk about fifteen minutes or so to get to Madeline's horse barn, unless my dad drove me. I hadn't asked him yet because, well, I just hadn't. I dressed in old jeans and a long-sleeved t-shirt. Who knows—I might have to clean up manure.

Downstairs, my mother was up, sitting at the kitchen table. The sight of her up at this time of the morning was a pleasant surprise. She wore an old bathrobe that was cinched at the waist, making her look rail thin. Her hair was stringy, greasy, and unkempt.

But, hey, she was up. That made me smile.

"Hi, Mom," I said softly. She'd been in bed for three days so I knew from past experience that loud noises startled her.

She sipped her coffee. "You're up early." A cigarette sat on the table beside a neon blue lighter.

"Not really." I poured myself coffee. "Thanks for making coffee," I said.

"Your dad made it."

"Is he gone?" My dad was a real estate agent who specialized in high-end properties. His face was on bus benches. He did well enough, financially, and when my mom couldn't work anymore after Faith died he took over as the main breadwinner. It worked. We only had to cut back a little.

She shrugged. "I'm not sure."

I put two teaspoons of sugar in my coffee and stirred it, the sound echoing through our silence.

"Are you…going somewhere?" Her hands shook as she picked up her mug.

This was the longest conversation we'd had in a week. "Yeah," I said, "I'm just going to…study with Anna."

I don't know why I lied. Except I guess I did know why. I didn't want to mention the word *horses* in front of her.

She nodded with a faraway look in her eyes. I let her be and got a bowl out of the cupboard and some cereal from the pantry. Once I had the cereal covered in milk, I sat down.

"Anna," she said. "How is she?"

"Good."

"How's school?"

For an entire week, I had wanted my mother to ask me a question about myself, any question, but not one about school.

"It's okay," I lied again.

"Good." She tapped her cigarette on the table. A huge part of me wanted to tell her smoking was bad for her, but I got that when she was down she needed to smoke, so I kept my mouth shut. Plus, she'd been a nurse—well, she still is, I guess—and she knows how bad smoking is for her. I wish she would go back to work. Could go back. I think it would be good for her. One day, she keeps saying. She was only supposed to be on a temporary medical leave but it has turned into a full year now. I have to believe her when she says *one day*.

"I'm sorry about last week," she said.

"It's okay," I said. "I understand."

"You're such a good boy. I don't know what I'd have done without you this past year."

I shovelled cereal in my mouth, my head bowed so I didn't have to look at her. How could I leave her to go to university?

"Good morning, everyone." My dad walked into the kitchen zipping up his grey sweatsuit jacket.

He went over to my mother and gently kissed her cheek. Then he went to the coffee pot and held it up. "Should I make more?"

"I'm good." I held up my mug.

"Me too," said my mom.

"You're up early," he said to me.

"Um, yeah." I had told him about the horses. He must have forgotten.

"He's studying with Anna," said my mother.

My dad frowned. I made a little slash across my throat and he gave a little nod. "I could use a ride," I said. "You look as if you're going out."

"I have to meet my personal trainer at the gym."

"Are you working today?" Often my dad worked on the weekend, showing potential buyers huge homes.

He shook his head. "I thought I'd take the day off. Unless something immediate comes up. I haven't had a Saturday off in years, it seems."

He glanced at the kitchen clock that hung above the table. "If I'm driving you somewhere we should get going. I don't want to miss my workout."

"I'm ready. We can go."

He snatched his keys off the key holder and slung his bag over his shoulder. Then he kissed the top of my mother's head. "I cut up fruit for you. It's on a plate in the fridge."

She nodded.

"I won't be long." He stroked her hair. "Can I get you anything?"

"I'm good," she said.

"Call me if you need me."

"I'll be fine." My mom stood and slipped her winter coat over her robe. With her cigarette and coffee she went out to the porch. I watched her huddle over her cigarette, flicking her lighter. When the cigarette sparked she drew in a huge breath of smoke, tilting her head back. One step at a time. At least smoking got her out of bed. I grabbed my coat too and followed my father out the front door.

Dad and I didn't talk as he backed out of the driveway. I wondered if he was also trying to rid his mind of the image of my mother, huddled over her cigarette. I stared out the window as the car backed up, bumped across the curb, and then jolted to a stop when my dad stomped on the brakes. He shoved it into drive and as it accelerated forward, he said, "Need some directions, bud."

"Yeah, I'm not going to Anna's."

"Right. I remember that now."

I nodded. "I'm not sure it's good to talk about horses around Mom."

"Gotcha." He paused. We remained silent for a few minutes, except for me saying *right* or *left*.

After a few turns he said, "Schoolwork any better?"

"Not really."

"Did you apply to any universities?"

"Not yet. I'm not sure if I even want to." I fiddled with the zipper on my jacket. "It's just…so much pressure."

"You don't have to, you know. Or you could apply and just see what happens. In the end, you only need to go if it's what you want. *Really* what you want. And I'm only asking because you always talked about university, about being a professor, from the time you were little."

"I *never* talked about being a professor," I said.

He looked at me with a silly grin on his face. "Okay, so not a professor but you wanted to be a hockey player with a scholarship."

"Well, I don't play hockey anymore."

"Yeah, and that's a shame. You were good."

"Things change." I had dreamed of a hockey scholarship until Faith died and I blew it by getting kicked out of a school for fighting and getting kicked off my hockey team. Then I just quit altogether.

"Life throws a lot of curves," he said.

"Sure does."

"There's nothing wrong with going to a community college, bud, if that's what *you* want," said my dad. "Just don't make decisions based on your mom and me, or anyone else. That's the most important thing. You do what's right for you. I went to university because your grandparents pushed me and I got a degree in history and now I sell real estate. And look at your Uncle Luke. He never went to university, and your grandma and grandpa were not happy about that, but he's got a really successful plumbing business. He's living a good life. There's community college, tech school, or you could even take a year off. Not everyone has to go to university right from high school. Just do what's right for you. You're young."

I didn't say anything. Being a real estate agent, Dad had the "gift of the gab" as my grandparents liked to say. But his ideas definitely gave me something to think about.

After a few minutes he asked, "So how are things going with Anna?"

"Good."

"You're young."

Second time he'd made *that* statement. "What's that supposed to mean?"

"Isn't she going away to California for school?"

"She hasn't decided yet but, yeah, that's looking like an option. She's been accepted to a few others too." Of course I knew what he meant by the *young* comment. And, of course, I'd thought about *us* next September. And she'd thought about *us* too. Were we going to even be an *us*?

"Love can be hard," he said.

More silence. Finally, we turned and headed down a lumpy, dirt road that led us to an old barn, but a beautiful wooden structure. Traces of graffiti adorned the one side and although it looked as if it had been around a while, it looked well built. Not decrepit at all. My dad cracked a smile and so did I.

"It's got character," he said. "I like it."

"Me too." I paused for a second. "Faith would have loved it."

"Yes, she would have." He really smiled and I liked how the corners of his eyes crinkled. That was a rare sight these days. "I can hear her squealing in the back seat." He actually laughed. But then I saw his watery eyes.

I put my hand on the door handle. "Thanks, Dad. I appreciate the ride. I can catch the bus home. Stay home with Mom."

I got out of the car and breathed in the fresh air. I took in my surroundings. Land stretched forward, horizons disappearing into the farmland. I liked the crisp day, the clear blue sky, and the bright winter sun that made the snow look pure. The beautiful sight was in stark contrast to Becky leaning against the barn, talking on her phone. I walked toward her. She saw me and said, "Hang on," to whoever she was talking to. She pulled her phone off her ear. "If you go inside you can get to the ring through the barn."

Then she went right back to her phone call.

I pulled open the barn door, sliding it across its runners, and entered into the empty barn, stalls lining each side. I guessed all the horses were outside already, which is where they should be. I saw the door at the other end and walked the length of the old barn, my footsteps loud on the wooden planks. The dim lighting of the building had this calming effect on me.

Once I was outside, I saw Madeline with the tiniest horse I'd ever seen. No wonder they were called miniatures. Faith would have loved them. Nostalgic feelings of being with Faith at the barn hit me hard, right in the solar plexus: the distinct smell, the sounds, the overall feel of sharing space with animals. I'd avoided horses and barns for this very reason. I watched for a second as Madeline fed the horse a carrot. When she stood, she stumbled a bit, her balance a bit off, but she grabbed onto the horse to right herself. The little animal looked up at her patiently, as if it knew it was supposed to help her.

I walked over to Madeline and I saw the joy on her face. *Move forward, I thought. This is not about Faith. It's about Madeline.*

Madeline introduced me to Willow and I reached down to pet her. I seriously had to reach down, not up or even over. Down. She was the teeniest horse. When she whinnied in pleasure, I found myself laughing. "She sure likes that," I said.

"Kiiisses too," she said.

I watched as Madeline leaned down and gently kissed Willow's nose. Willow, loving every minute, blinked her eyes in pleasure.

Madeline and I talked for a few minutes and then suddenly I just blurted out, "Faith would have loved it here."

"Diiid she riiide big hooorses?"

"Yeah. But she would have loved these little ones." For some reason, I felt comfortable talking to Madeline about Faith. We chatted for a few more minutes about Faith. Longest I'd talked about her since the one therapy session I'd gone to.

"Thanks, Madeline," I said, "for inviting me here."

"Yooou're welcooome," she said in a happy voice.

"And now that I'm here, what do we need to do?"

"The diiirty wooork." She grinned. "Cleeeaning the staaalls."

"I'm game," I said.

"Gooood. Becky haaates cleaning the staaalls."

"I bet. She's off the hook because I'm here to help today."

We finished the stalls and I hauled out the wheelbarrow. I was bringing it back in when a tall, slim woman walked over to me.

"You must be Justin," she said. Her smile was warm and her eyes bright. She rubbed sweat off her forehead with her sleeve and left a streak of mud across her dark skin.

"I am," I replied. "Nice to meet you."

"Looks like Madeline's put you to work."

"She drives a hard bargain. But, honestly, I don't mind. I used to do this all the time."

"I saw on your volunteer form that you have experience with horses."

"I do."

"That's helpful to us. I don't know if Madeline explained much but we use the minis for therapy. Madeline started visiting for therapy but now she's my best volunteer."

By now, Madeline was beside me and she held Willow by her lead. Madeline smiled at the compliment and stroked Willow.

"We've even had a few adults who have come in for therapy," said Tonya, "and we take the horses out in the community as well. They love going to hospitals and nursing homes."

"Wow," I said. "That's cool. I've never been around these little guys before. To be honest, I didn't even know this kind of therapy existed." I leaned over and petted Willow again and she nuzzled into me before she snorted.

Madeline laughed. "She doooesn't like beeeing caaalled a guy. She's a priiincess."

"Well, I guess she told me," I said, laughing as well.

"You're in for a treat," said Tonya. "They are such smart little animals. Once you start volunteering today, I promise, you'll want to come back." She paused. "Is Becky here too? Speaking of volunteers…" She looked around.

I glanced at the door too. "I think she's outside on her phone."

Tonya shook her head. "Okay. It is what it is. I guess not everyone is in love like Madeline and I are. We need to get started. Once you take that wheelbarrow back in, come out to the ring and join us."

Madeline took Willow and started to walk her around while I put the wheelbarrow back where it belonged. Then I came back to the ring.

I saw a teeny tiny horse, smaller than Willow, and she was dressed up in what looked like colourful gypsy clothes. There were a few kids petting the horse and she was lapping up the attention.

"Thaaat's Daaaphne," said Madeline to me. "Sheee's ooonly ooone."

Tonya walked over to Madeline and me. "There's a little girl named Maala coming today," she said. "She has cerebral palsy. Justin, if you can help her mother hold her on Willow, then Madeline can walk her around. Very slowly. She's four, a tiny four, and a real trooper. And she loves the horses, especially Willow."

"Sure," I said. "I'll do anything."

"There they are now," said Tonya, motioning her head toward a lady pushing a wheelchair through a gate.

"Okay, you guys are on your own," said Tonya. "I'm heading over to get Cowboy ready. He's our biggest male." Tonya walked away at a good clip, her rubber boots sloshing through the mud and wet snow.

For a few seconds I watched Maala's mother push her wheelchair through the snow and dirt, not an easy task. Then I hurried over. "Can I help? Maybe if we carried the chair?"

"That would be wonderful," she said.

I held out my hand. "Oh, by the way, my name's Justin and I'm a new volunteer. I'm here with Madeline."

"Oh, we just love Madeline. She's been so good to Maala. It's nice to meet you Justin." She shook my hand. "I'm Heather."

I crouched down and looked at Maala. "You ready for a ride?"

She tilted her head and smiled from ear to ear.

We lifted the chair, getting it out of the snow, and after a few steps, set it down.

Her mother lifted her up. "I can take her if you want," I said. "Or help you."

"It's okay. I'm used to carrying her."

Madeline was waiting for us by Willow, and Maala's face lit up when she saw her.

"Hiii, Maaaala," said Madeline. "Wiiillow is haaappy to see yooou."

I watched as Willow moved right over to Maala, burrowing her nose into her neck. Willow whinnied and Maala squealed in delight. Willow got up on her hind legs, putting her hooves on Heather's knees, which allowed Maala to hug her around the neck. Just like a dog. A deep belly laugh erupted from inside me.

The rest of the morning flew by. When the riding was over for the kids, Madeline took Willow's lead off of her and went inside the barn, coming out with a little tray of brushes, and Becky. Who looked absolutely miserable. I hadn't even noticed that Becky had stayed away from the horses until now. That's how engrossed I was.

"So, did you have fun?" she asked me, sarcastically.

"I did," I said. "Too bad you didn't join in."

She rolled her eyes before she turned to Madeline. "Maddie, Dad texted and said he'll be here in twenty minutes."

Madeline turned to me. "Yooou shooould meeeet my daaad."

"Sure," I answered.

I helped Madeline brush Willow and Daphne, and then we cleaned their hooves. All little jobs I'd done before. Becky didn't do the hooves (said it was *the worst job ever*) but did help with brushing. Then her phone pinged.

She quickly pulled it out of her pocket. "Dad is going be here in two minutes," she said.

We put everything away and said goodbye to Tonya.

Walking through the barn, I followed behind Becky and Madeline.

Madeline's legs wobbled as she walked, and her footsteps were loud as she clunked herself forward. She'd told me she had to focus when she walked, telling herself "one foot in front of the other." Side-by-side, Becky walked with Madeline, her arm linked in hers. Becky didn't rush Madeline but moved along at her pace.

So the girl does have a soft side.

Once outside, I saw a man about my height, but slighter, standing by a grey Audi. He smiled, waved, and made his way over to us. Madeline and Becky both waved back and picked up their pace, and when Madeline stumbled a little, Becky held her up. They looked happy to see each other, the three of them, and a stab of pain hit my chest. My mom used to be happy to see me and Faith after a day at the barn. Being with the horses had made me forget about what was at home.

I shook my head. *Not about you, Justin.*

I moved forward, until I was standing beside Madeline.

"Daaad," said Madeline. "Thiiis is Juuustin. He's myyy Beeest Buddyyy."

I stuck out my hand. "Pleased to meet you."

"Madeline has talked a lot about you." He shook my hand with a firm grip. "It's a pleasure to meet you. That Best Buddies program has sure been good for Madeline."

"Yeah," I said. "I enjoy it too." I looked at Madeline. "She plays a mean card game."

"Juuustin does caaard triiicks," she said with a giggle.

"Card tricks. That's good," said her father.

"Heee liiiked the hooorses," said Madeline.

Madeline's father winked at her. "I have a surprise for you girls tomorrow," he said.

"What is it?" Becky asked.

"You'll see. If I tell you it won't be a surprise." Becky actually smiled at his joke. Whoa. This guy might be made of magic.

"We should get going," he said to Madeline and Becky.

"Yeah, me too," I said. "My dad's picking me up."

I waited for them to leave before I started walking down the lane that led to the road and the bus stop.

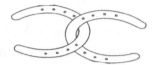

I arrived home just after one o'clock and my mother was still dressed in her pajamas, but she was still up and I wondered if she'd sat at the table for the entire time I was gone. Had she eaten? Or just smoked a pack of cigarettes?

"I'm starving." I opened the fridge. "You want me to make us some lunch?" Although, after looking in the fridge, I wondered how that would be possible. Vegetables and more vegetables. I wanted a sandwich. Peanut butter and jam perhaps. Cheese on bread. Did we even have bread?

"I think I need to nap," she said.

I turned to look at her. Blue bags rimmed her eyes. "Is Dad home?"

She shook her head. "He was here but he left to go to a meeting and get groceries for dinner tonight."

"I thought he didn't have any meetings scheduled for today."

"It came up suddenly," she said. "He wasn't going to go but I told him to." She waved her hand in front of her face.

"If he's getting groceries, I'm going to text him with some suggestions. He needs to get some good stuff. And not just vegetables."

I glanced at her and thought I saw a little smile. Just a little one. I wanted to tell her about the horses but I wasn't sure if that would make her upset. She got up from the table and kissed my cheek as she was going by me.

"You and your dad are so good to me," she said.

CHAPTER SEVEN
MADELINE

My dad's house is so different from my mom's. He was the one who moved out, leaving Mom with the house Becky and I were kids in, and he bought a brand new two-bedroom place where everything was on the one floor except the basement. He did that for me. It had some type of countertop and kitchen appliances that my mom always said she wanted but he wouldn't buy for her. Something about the stone on the counter and the stainless steel fridge made her mutter under her breath. Since it was only two bedrooms, Becky and I shared, but the room was big and we had two single beds and a dresser for clothes we wanted to leave there. And we had a television in our room but that was something we weren't supposed to tell Mom. The house also had a big room in the basement with another huge television because Dad liked to watch sports, and we hooked up our computers to watch Netflix. In some ways, for me anyway, Dad's house was an escape. For Becky it was also an escape but in a different way.

We spent the afternoon lazing around downstairs, watching, of all things, horror movies, including an old one called *Carrie*. Becky gave me a big spiel about how it was written by Stephen King, her new favourite author. Go figure. Becky hated reading, and she used to hate horror movies and any show of blood, until her new friends came along.

When the movie ended, she sat up and curled her legs into her chest. "That mother was so freaky in that movie. She grabbed a huge knife and stabbed her daughter."

"It's juuust a mooovie," I said.

"Yeah, I know," she said. "But it makes you think."

"Not reeeally."

She turned to me and her eyes looked wild almost.

"You're geeetting weeeird," I said.

Instead of answering me, she snatched her phone off the table and wrote a text. Within seconds her phone pinged back.

I glanced at my phone on the table. It almost never pings at all. I don't have a lot of friends. I had friends, before and even after the accident, for a few years anyway, but when we hit high school I wasn't the girl other kids wanted to hang out with. Too much work, I guess. Too slow; too uncoordinated. My brain takes time.

But I have my horses. So I told myself I didn't care.

And now I have Justin and all the kids in the Best Buddies group.

After her phone pinged a few more times, Becky turned to me. "Tonight, you have to leave our bedroom window open."

"Iiit's cooold."

"I'm going out."

"Doooes Daaad knooow?"

"No. And you're not going to tell him. We're going to go to bed early and I'm going out the window, and when I come home I will come in through the window."

"Juuust ask Daaad if you caaan go ooout."

"Mom told him I was grounded for leaving the barn the other night. How dumb is that? It's not like I was even drunk when I came home at eight o'clock. Seriously, eight o'clock! I don't think Mom was *ever* a teenager."

"Dooo yoooour frieeends driiink?"

Becky didn't answer me but hugged a cushion tight, staring straight ahead. I had no idea what she was thinking. So weird.

"Hey, girls!" My dad's voice bellowed down. "Come on up and see what Chinese food you want to order."

"You'll do this for me?" she asked. "And next time I'll take you with me."

"Nooo, thaaanks." I got up and went upstairs.

In the kitchen, my dad had the menu already up on his iPad and also a brochure on the table. "Pick what you want," he said.

I sat down in front of the iPad and started clicking through the menu. Becky leaned over my shoulder.

"Sweet-and-sour pork," said Becky.

"I like those dried ribs," said my dad. "Anything you want, Madeline?"

I couldn't think fast enough. There were things I liked. *What were they?*

"You like lemon chicken," said Becky.

"Yeeeah, lemon chiiicken," I said.

"Couple more," said Dad. "I can eat them as leftovers tomorrow."

We completed the menu and Dad called in the order. Dad let us each have a can of pop, which, of course, is a no-no at Mom's house.

"Tell me about school," he said as we waited.

"Sucks," said Becky. "What else you want to know?"

"You need to try harder," he said. "And I'm serious."

Becky hung her head. Dad rarely reprimanded her.

"I gooot an A on myyy poooem," I said.

"You're so good, Maddie," said Becky. "Like, you should get published somewhere."

"I'm nooot thaaat good."

"Can I read your poem?" my dad asked.

I thought about the one that I just wrote. I didn't want him to read that one. "I wrooote one abooout Beeest Buuuddies. Yoooou caaan reeead it."

"I look forward to it," he said. "That group has been good for you."

"I liiike it."

"Justin seemed like a nice kid," said Dad. "He's a little old for you though." He winked at me.

"Daaad," I said. "He's myyy frieeend."

"And boring," said Becky. "The guy never smiles."

"Yeees, he doooes. And heee's fuuunny. Yooour friends dooon't smile eeeither," I said. "Theeey weeear blaaack and waaalk like zooommbies."

Dad turned to Becky. "How come I haven't met these new friends?"

Becky shrugged. Then she said, "Hey, you said we get a surprise tomorrow. What is it?"

"It wouldn't be a surprise if I told you, now, would it?" He grinned.

"Cooome ooon," I said.

We harassed my dad about telling us the surprise until the doorbell rang. Dad got up from the table. "I'll get it. You girls get the plates out."

We were halfway through eating when Dad said, "Did you girls want to watch the hockey game with me tonight?"

"Yeah, right," said Becky. She faked a yawn. "I think I'll do some homework and read for a bit." Then she looked me right in the eyes. "Maddie, you want to watch some TV in our bedroom? Like *Pretty Little Liars* or *Switched at Birth*? We could have a little pajama party."

Thankfully, my mouth was full of food so I didn't have to answer. When I first came out of my coma, after my accident, I had a feeding tube in my stomach and couldn't eat. It took me months to learn how to eat again and I had a lot of trouble with swallowing so I drooled and choked all the time. I wore bibs. At first, my mom fed me food with a straw. Then I graduated to the spoon because if I used a fork, I'd accidentally stab myself. It was a huge deal when I graduated to a fork. Now, I could eat but I wasn't supposed to eat and talk at the same time.

My lack of answering was nothing unusual. Dad didn't pick up on a thing.

Becky acted like the model daughter and helped do the dishes, then we were given the green light to go to our room.

"I'll be downstairs," said Dad. "Oh, and I bought ice cream. Häagen-Dazs, chocolate and peanut butter, and some other kind with caramel cones mashed up in it."

"Awesome," said Becky.

As if she was having ice cream.

Becky and I went to our room and she shut the door tight. "If Dad comes to the door just say you're changing or...I'm in the bathroom." We had our own bathroom (my mom called it an "ensuite") in our room, which was really nice and handy.

"He always knocks if the door is shut, so make sure you keep it shut."

I didn't speak.

Of course, Becky continued talking. "But what would be best is if you would go down around ten or eleven and say I fell asleep so he doesn't come up to say goodnight."

"Whaaat if I dooon't want tooo?"

"Come on, Maddie. Help me out here. You've got your horses and I've got my friends."

I flopped on my bed and turned on the television.

"Just think," she said as she undressed, "you can watch whatever you want tonight."

I flicked through the channels as she put on her all-black ensemble, including black eyeliner and lipstick.

"Thaaat looooks groooss," I said.

"That's your opinion."

"Wheeere are yoooou goooing?" I asked. "A paaarty?"

"Kind of."

What that meant, I wasn't sure, and I didn't want to ask. When she was ready, complete with a black toque and black gloves, she quietly hoisted up the window and slipped out. I heard her land and went over to the window, watching her shadow sneak through the bushes and out to the clearing. Once she was out of sight, I closed the window a little because the room was freezing. I would open it later, before I went to bed.

At around ten I went to the kitchen and got a bowl of ice cream. Then I went downstairs.

"Whooo's wiiinning?" I asked.

"The Oilers," he said. "About time too."

He was a big fan ever since Wayne Gretzky played for them years ago, before I was even born. A signed jersey even hung on the wall in his basement. In his own house, he did what he wanted.

"Sit down," he said. "I can change the station. This game is all but over anyway." He moved over on the sofa to give me room. "Where's Becky?"

"Sleeeeping," I said. Thankfully, all the lights were off so he couldn't see my lying eyes.

"I guess she's been acting out a bit." He flicked through the stations. "Tell me what you want to watch."

"She haaas new frieeends," I said. I sat down on the sofa and he handed me the remote.

"Pick something," he said.

I'd flicked through a few stations when he asked, "What are these new friends like?"

I shrugged. "Theeey wear blaaack." I settled on an old episode of *Friends*, knowing my dad would like it.

"What happened to all those kids you girls used to hang around with? That Sarah and Amy? You played with them through elementary school. I thought they still lived in the neighbourhood."

I thought about Sarah and Amy. They *used to* be my friends. But things changed. In grade eight they started hanging out with Becky more than me. Now they just hang out with their volleyball friends.

"Madeline?"

"I'm sooorry," I said, snapping back to the present. "Whaaat did yoooou aaask?"

"Sarah and Amy. You don't see them anymore."

"Theeey haaang ooout wiiith sooome ooother kiiids. Theeey dooon't liiike Becky's new frieeends," I said. "And theeey don't waaant to haaang around with meee wiiithout Beeecky."

"I'm sorry, sweetie."

"It's oookay, Daaad. I've got sooome frieeends in the Beeest Buddies prograaam."

High school was tough, no doubt about it. Mom kept telling me to give it a chance but no one liked someone who talked slow and had strange emotions and was uncoordinated and stupid at math.

"That's good then. You need friends."

"Hooorses too," I said.

"You're going to love tomorrow's surprise," he said.

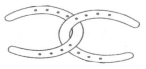

Just after midnight, I heard a rapping on the window. Oh no, I had forgotten to reopen it. I got up as quickly as I could but my balance was off and I tripped.

"Maddie!" Becky's voice sounded like a growl outside the window.

I pulled myself up, using my bed post, and went to the window. Once I pried it open, she crawled through and fell to the floor with a thump.

"*Shhh*," I said, alarmed. Was she drunk?

The smell of cigarettes wafted through the room.

"You were supposed to leave it open," she said.

"It's sooo laaate," I said.

She didn't sound drunk. And I couldn't smell anything but cigarette smoke. I knew her friends drank because they talked about it at school.

"It's not *that* late. I was the first to go home. I'm like a baby who always has to go home."

"Weeere you smoooking?"

"Just one," she said.

"It's baaad for yooou."

"So?"

"Wheeere weeere you?"

"The park."

"Weeere they driiinking?"

Becky shrugged. "Yeah, maybe—who cares? Lots of kids drink. We're like the *only ones* who don't."

"I caaan't. Caaan you imagiiine how uncoordiiinaaated I wooould beee?"

I thought she might laugh when I said that but she didn't. Even in the dark, I could see something was not right. She seemed sad or something.

All she said was, "I know *you* can't. But that doesn't mean *I* can't. Maddie, we're just different right now. We want different things. And that's okay."

"Dooo you waaant to driiink?"

She shrugged. "I dunno. My friends do. It might be fun. They laugh a lot when they're drunk. Or...maybe I just want to forget stuff. Getting drunk helps that, from what I hear."

"Whaaat stuff?"

"Nothing." She started to undress. "I'm tired. I'm going to bed."

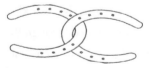

In the morning, Dad woke us up bright and early by knocking on our door. "Time to get up," he said.

Becky rolled over and curled into a small ball, ignoring him. I got up, feeling a bit dazed. What day was it? I looked at my phone. Sunday. I glanced at my notes app. All it said was *surprise* and *wear outdoor clothes*.

I rubbed my temples. What had happened last night? Sometimes my brain took time to get it together in the morning. I had to think hard, concentrate. I looked around the room. Coping skills. Becky's black clothes were lying all over the floor.

I saw the window. What was it about the window?

"Beeecky," I said. "Whyyy aaam I thiiinking abooout the wiiindow?"

She groaned. "You were supposed to leave it open last night and you didn't."

Then I sort of remembered. Little pieces. "Yoou caaame hooome laaate."

"Not that late." She moaned.

I heard Dad's shower going so I got out of bed. "Beeecky," I said. "Tiiime to geeet up. Weee geeet a suuurprise."

She sat up and rubbed her eyes. "Better be a good surprise. It's too early."

I shook my head. Whatever. I got dressed and went downstairs.

"Good morning," said my dad in this chipper voice. His hair was wet from his shower and he had a huge grin on his face. I saw that the table was set for breakfast. I could smell toast. Dad was the king of big breakfasts: eggs, toast, bacon, hash browns. And he made the best omelettes.

After the toast had popped up and he had buttered it and put it in front of us, he started tapping his hands on the table like a drumroll. "So the surprise is…."

"Why are you making that noise?" Becky grumbled as she walked into the kitchen.

"Drumroll. For the surprise." He raised his eyebrows up and down.

"Seriously, Dad." She shook her head.

I grinned at him. I liked it when my dad was fun. "Teeell uuus," I said.

"I'm taking you to see real horses today," he said proudly.

"Reeeally?" I think I squealed.

"*That's* the surprise?" Becky flopped into the kitchen chair.

"I thought you'd be thrilled," he said.

"Horses stink."

"I'm thriiilled," I said.

"Trust me, Becky, it'll be fun. We are going out this morning. Then we can have a late lunch, and I'll drop you back at your mom's."

Mumbling and moaning, like seriously mumbling and moaning, Becky got ready and we all got in the car. She didn't even call shotgun so I got to sit in the front. She sat on the back and was on her phone the entire drive. We drove for at least forty-five minutes before Dad pulled into a ranch.

"This is going to be a private trail ride for the three of us," said Dad.

"Can I just sleep in the car?" Becky asked from the back seat.

"No, Becky. You can't," said Dad.

We all put on helmets then individually we were introduced to our horses. Mine was a beautiful chocolate brown and white palomino named Gabby. I thought she was gorgeous. I rubbed her nose like I did with Willow and she responded by burrowing her head into me. I heard my dad talking to the owner of the ranch, Isobel.

"She's a natural. Horses love her," he said.

"I can see that."

Isobel explained everything about the trail ride and then it was time to go. Isobel helped me get on my horse. One day I would learn to mount a horse by myself. Once I was up, I sat tall and my entire body tingled with excitement. The sky was overcast but the temperature hovered a few degrees above freezing. I thought it was perfect. I followed directly behind Isobel, making sure I wasn't too close, just like she said. She had explained to me how to hold the reins and how to make Gabby walk using them.

We went slowly and I liked that. We travelled away from the ranch and into the woods. Becky was behind me and thankfully she'd stopped mumbling. Dad was at the rear.

We walked and walked and then we came to a stream. Isobel turned and said, "Let's give them a drink." She slid off her horse.

Suddenly, I could feel my heart beating through my clothes. How was I going to get off? I'd never done this before. I was uncoordinated. My brain started pounding. My emotions were getting away from me and I didn't want them to.

No. No. Please. Not now.

"Maddie needs help," said Becky.

Isobel came over to me and my horse and gently put her hand on my leg. "You can do this."

Immediately, I calmed down. Slowly, she explained everything I needed to do, and then I slid down and off my horse. I landed and didn't fall. Gabby whinnied and I breathed. I slowly led her over to the creek, concentrating on walking and leading, and we got there. Gabby lowered her head and drank.

When we were back at the ranch after riding for almost two hours, I turned to my dad and said, "Taaake a piiicture. I waaant to seeend it to Juuustin."

"Ooo-la-la," said Becky. "I'll take it."

I ignored Becky's comment, and smiled as she clicked away, taking lots of photos for me. Then I dismounted like a pro, according to my dad.

"Thaaank you, Isooobel." I turned to my father. "Thaaanks, Daaad."

"Come back." Isobel touched my shoulder. "Anytime."

We went for lunch, and Becky and I both ate burgers and fries. All the way back to Mom's, I talked about the horses.

I didn't care if Becky didn't have as much fun as me. And I texted the photo to Justin. He texted right back. And we went back and forth. He said he wanted to show me photos of his sister on the horses she rode. We decided to meet at lunch on Monday.

The day had been wonderful until Dad dropped us off.

"You took her *where*?" Mom asked Dad.

"She did fine," said Becky. "Leave it alone. Bye, Dad. Thanks. See you Wednesday." She blew him a kiss as she went in the house, and I was left alone with Mom and Dad.

"It was good for her," said my dad.

"I wooore a heeelmet," I said. "It waaas so amaaazing, Mooom." I hated when they talked in the third person around me. When I was in the hospital, people talked about me all the time in front of me, as if I wasn't even there.

"And you had a helmet on when you fell off your bike," said my mother. "You may not remember but I do."

Why did she have to bring this up?

"Leah, come on," said my dad.

My mother shook her head at him. "I actually don't have that *big* an issue with her horseback riding. What I do have an issue with is you not telling me. You should have let me know."

"I didn't think you'd let her go."

"That's ridiculous."

"Mooom. Daaad. Stooop."

My mom turned to me. "Madeline, maybe it would be better if you went in the house. I need to talk to your dad in private."

Since I knew what was coming, I went inside and directly to my room where I shut the door. Locked away, I couldn't hear them fight. I wrecked our family by falling off my bike. Me. I had done this to our family.

My head started pounding. And pounding. And pounding. I started hitting and hitting the side of my skull to make it stop. And when I couldn't stop, I cried out for Becky.

She was at my side in seconds, rocking me back and forth. "It's okay, Maddie. It's okay. I'm here."

CHAPTER EIGHT
JUSTIN

After Madeline sent me all those pictures of her on the horse over the weekend, I couldn't wait to see her at lunch on Monday. All morning I looked forward to showing her photos of Faith, photos I had dug up from a box I'd hid under my bed. I'd never shown Anna any of these photos. They were my precious memories that I'd wanted to keep to myself, until I met Madeline.

Another test back and another crappy 68%. Again. This sort of mark wouldn't even come close to helping me get into a good university. I crumpled it up and threw it in my backpack.

At lunch, I rushed to get to the cafeteria. And bumped into Anna.

"I'm meeting with Madeline," I said.

"I'll join you guys."

"Um, she wanted me to go over a few things with her. Some English stuff. She might not want someone else there because she really struggles and I know it's embarrassing for her. Why don't you meet us in like, half an hour?" I wasn't one for stringing together a lot of sentences so this was like I'd just read Anna a novel. Why was I running off at the mouth? I was acting like I was twelve instead of seventeen.

"Okay," she said.

I leaned into her and gave her a kiss, something I rarely did in the hallway.

"Wow," she smiled coyly at me. "I liked that."

"Later." I winked.

"I'll hold you to that," she said.

Madeline waited for me at the cafeteria door and we walked in together. Once we sat down at an out-of-the-way table, I pulled out my photos. "I wanted to show you these after you sent me the photo yesterday," I said.

I slid a photo of Faith on the horse she liked the best, a palomino, over to Madeline.

"Yooour siiister is preeetty," she said. "The hooorse looks like Gaaabby. The ooone I rooode yeeesterday."

"Wow," I said. "Great job saying *yesterday*!"

She smiled at me.

"This one looks like the horse you rode. That's why I brought this photo." I glanced down at the photo and Faith looked so happy, just like Madeline had in her photo. "Did you like the riding?" I asked her.

"It waaas aaawesome. Buuut I still looove Wiiillow." She pointed to my photos. "Shooow me mooore."

We ate our lunch as we looked at photos. I had leftover Chinese food and she had some sort of salad that looked like the stuff my dad ate.

Then she saw one of Faith and my mom standing by a horse. She pointed to my mother. "Sheee's preeetty too," she said. "Theeey look aliiike."

I nodded, staring at the photo. She *had been* pretty. And Faith *had been* the spitting image of her. They'd had a deep bond and my mother had done everything to help her with her autism and support her. She never tried to change her and I had liked that. She'd also gone out of her way to go to conferences and read books, and she took her to classes designed for kids with autism. I went to the classes with her sometimes too. But she hadn't been able to control what the kids said to her at school. Or what happened when she went to rehab. Faith had outsmarted everyone.

"She's, um, had a hard since Faith died." I don't know why I was opening up to Madeline but somehow it felt okay.

"Myyy mooom too," she said. "And I diiidn't even diiie."

"She misses her." I paused. "A lot. We all do."

"I'm sooorry," she said. "Maaaybe Faith and I cooould haaave been frieeends."

My eyes almost welled up with tears. It took me a few seconds to gather myself together before I said, "She would have liked you."

"Cooome see the hooorses agaaain."

"I will," I said. "I'll come Wednesday."

"Briiing your mooom."

My mom?

"Oh, um, I don't know about that," I said. I gathered up the photos and put them back in the envelope. "Let's work on your English."

We'd finished one question when Anna joined us and she was even better at helping with schoolwork than I was. And Madeline wasn't embarrassed at all. I listened to the two of them but my mind was elsewhere. Like with my mother.

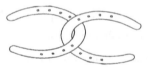

All day I thought about what Madeline had said. Maybe I should approach my mother, ask her to join us. Dad would have to drive us though. She wouldn't be strong enough to catch the bus and walk. I'd talk to Dad first.

I got home after school and actually did some homework as I waited for my dad to come home. My mother sat at the table with me for a little while and it gave me hope. Then she said she was going up to have a bath. I wanted to tell her to wash her hair, but I kept my mouth shut.

Dad came home just after Mom went upstairs. He was wearing what looked to be a new suit with a crisp white shirt, and he had a new haircut and smelled of body spray. He looked good.

"Where's your mom?" he asked.

"Having a bath."

"That's great!"

"Yeah." I paused. Then I blurted out, "I want to talk to you about something."

"Sure," he said.

"You know those horses I went to see—the miniature ones that are used for therapy?"

"What about them?" He pulled chicken out of the fridge.

"I think Mom could benefit from them. I want to ask her to come out with me. What do you think? You'd have to drive us."

He turned to look at me. "I think that's a great idea. And, of course, I'd drive you. That's a given."

"Do you think she will? I'm worried it might set her back."

He clicked his tongue, frowning as if he was thinking hard. "Maybe...we need to be more proactive. Push her just a little. This is a good suggestion."

He nodded his head. Then he started cutting chicken. "Can you cut veggies? I thought I'd make a stir fry."

"Sure," I said.

"Your mom mention anything about eating with us?"

"I didn't ask her."

He put his knife down. "I will."

Fifteen minutes later he came back down, now dressed in a Nike sweatsuit that also looked new. After losing forty pounds I guess he did need new clothes. He put up his thumb and said, "She's coming down."

"Did you ask her about the horses?"

"I thought we could do it together over dinner. You game?"

I nodded. "Absolutely."

Inside I could feel my stomach churning. What if she said no? What if the thought of it was too much for her? What if it stirred up memories that were too hard to handle?

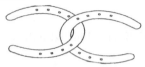

The next morning, snow fell from the sky, large flakes that seemed to be sticking to the ground. I trudged through it and managed to get to my bus stop on time. If this kept up we might get out of school early for a snow day.

As soon as I got to school, I saw Madeline. Was she waiting for me? She looked excited about something.

"What's up?" I asked. "You're wearing a grin bigger than a house."

"It's snooowing," she said.

"You thinking snow day?"

"If iiit snooows, Tonya wiiill geeet out the sleeeighs."

"Sleighs?"

"The hooorses puuull sleighs and the kiiids riiide in theeem. Meee too. It's sooo fun."

"Oh, wow. That sounds cool."

"Is yooour mom coooming?"

I held up my thumb. "Yes! My dad and I asked her last night and she said she would come on Saturday."

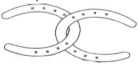

Wednesday night after school there was a foot of snow on the ground but all the roads were cleared. Buses wouldn't be slow or late today. I glanced at my phone, noticing that I only had five minutes to get to my bus stop. I'd even worn boots knowing I had to walk to the barn after my bus ride.

As I headed out of the school, Anna ran up behind me.

"Hey," she said, puffing. "You need a ride home?"

"That's okay. I'm going to the barn with Madeline." I kept moving at a good clip.

"By bus?" She was still sort of jogging to keep up. "Hey, slow down."

"I can't. I don't want to miss it."

"I'll drive you," she said. "I'd love to see those horses anyways. I probably can't stay the entire time because I have to tutor but I can sure drive you over."

That made me stop. I did want Anna to see the horses. "That would be great. You're going to love them."

We backtracked to her car and she started it, letting it run for a few minutes to warm up.

"This will be fun," she said.

"Yeah. It's an interesting concept."

She put her car in reverse. "Oh, I've got some news on the Evening of Friendship," she said. "The photo booth is a go. Everyone is going to have so much fun with it."

I laughed. "Can you imagine Erika?"

"Harrison probably won't want to put any of the costumes on but I'm going to get him to *try* a pair of those crazy glasses. I'm going to bring sanitary wipes. That might help. And if not, no big deal."

"I saw him talking to Madeline the other day in the hall," I said.

"Really? He was asking me questions about her." She raised her eyebrows up and down.

We talked about the event and the logistics behind it, which Anna was working on for the rest of the way to the barn. Only one part of the parking lot at the barn had been cleared of snow and I wondered if Tonya did everything there was to do.

After Anna parked, we walked through the barn to the ring and that's when I saw the sleigh. It looked like one of those old-fashioned ones with the curled runners, like a small chariot. But it was miniature, like the horses, which were all out, prancing around in the snow.

Anna tugged on my jacket. "Oh, my goodness. They are *sooooo* cute."

"I know."

I took Anna's hand. "Come on, I'll introduce you to Tonya, the owner, and Willow, Madeline's favourite horse."

We walked down the ramp and Madeline was at the bottom with Willow.

"Hi, Madeline," said Anna. "Justin's been telling me so much about these horses that I had to come see them for myself."

"Thiiis is Wiiillow," said Madeline with pride.

"She's beautiful. Can I pet her?"

"Sheee loooves atteeention."

Anna reached out and gave Willow a weak little pat on the nose. I realized she probably didn't have a lot of experience with horses.

"Don't worry," I said. "You won't hurt her."

"She is lovely," said Anna.

Madeline looked up at me, her eyes full of excitement. "Diiid yooou see the sleeeigh?"

"I did," I said. "I can't wait to see how it works." I looked across at Tonya who was untangling what looked like a bridle. "It looks as if she needs help."

"I think I'll stay here with Madeline," said Anna, pointing to her little shoes that weren't designed for snow and muck. "I can't stay long but how about I take photos?"

Tonya was placing the bridle over Cowboy's head as I walked over to her. It looked complicated with the little eye protectors and head gear.

"Need help?" I asked.

"Yes," she said gratefully. "Right now, I'm trying to hook Cowboy up to this sleigh. We have some smaller sleighs as well that are like toboggans and they're better for the little ones. I'll put the littler horses with them. They're not quite as difficult." She held up the bridle. "This one has a lot of pieces."

"We can do it," I said. "Oh, I brought my girlfriend, Anna. She just gave me a ride over. I hope that's okay. She isn't staying long and she hasn't filled out the volunteer form but she just wants to take some photos."

"No problem. She can also help us untangle these reins without filling out the volunteer form."

"She doesn't exactly have the right footwear," I said.

Tonya looked over at Anna and Madeline. Then she called out, "Madeline. Get Anna a pair of boots from the barn."

I wanted to burst out laughing when I saw Anna in knee-high rubber boots slopping over to us but I didn't.

After introductions, we all helped Tonya sort out the reins and get Cowboy hooked up to the antique sleigh. Anna worked her logical magic and I could tell Tonya appreciated her efficiency. Soon we had the sleigh up and running as well as the smaller toboggans.

"Justin, I have to go," said Anna.

"Thanks for your help," said Tonya.

"*Next time* I'll take pictures," she said to Tonya, smiling.

When Maala arrived, I went over to Heather to help her get Maala into the sleigh. The look on Maala's face as Willow pulled her around was worth a million photos. Her mother watched from the fence and every time Maala went by, she waved and Maala waved back like she was the Queen of England. Heather snapped photo after photo.

Becky was also helping today by walking Cowboy around with a little boy in the sleigh. She actually seemed to be enjoying herself.

The sun started dipping down, and I suddenly felt the chill of the night air. Tonya started to wrap up the afternoon and parents left with their children.

Soon it was just the volunteers left. Tonya would need help with the disassembling of the bridles as well. I had a walk and a bus to catch but I didn't care about the time.

"Madeline," said Tonya. "You want Cowboy to pull you? Last ride of the day."

"Can he pull Becky too?"

"I don't see why not. He's pretty strong."

Madeline and Becky got in the sleigh and, on cue, Cowboy walked forward.

I pulled my phone out of my pocket and started taking pictures. They both wore huge smiles and were giggling about something.

"It's good to see those two girls having fun," said Tonya.

Moments later, Madeline's mother pulled up and came to stand by us.

"Hi, Leah," said Tonya. "You're just in time."

I watched as Tonya put her hand on Leah's shoulder. "She's so good with the horses. She was so excited about her trail ride on the weekend."

"I know." Leah nodded.

"Okay, girls," said Tonya. "Time to call it a day."

Leah glanced at her watch. "We should get home."

"I neeeed to heeelp cleeean up," said Madeline.

"Really, Maddie?" said Becky. "We're getting off easy here."

"It's okay, Madeline," said Tonya, wagging her finger at Becky. "You can go now. I can finish up."

"I'll help," I said.

Tonya looked at Madeline and said, "Why don't you fill in the board inside the barn for me. We can take care of the horses."

Madeline nodded.

After Madeline had left with Becky and her mom, I helped Tonya to unhook Cowboy and take his bridle off. We didn't speak but worked side by side. I also helped with the sleighs because they needed to be carried to the side of the barn.

Finally, after the sleighs were put away and the horses were happy with their snack of hay, I said, "I'd like to bring my mother here one day, maybe Saturday. Would that be okay?"

"Sure. I can give you a volunteer sheet for her to fill out."

"Actually," I said hesitantly, "she'd come for therapy."

"What kind of therapy?"

"Um, depression." I stared down at my boot.

Tonya put her hand on my shoulder. "You're one good kid."

We finished up and I grabbed my backpack and headed outside. Darkness had settled in and I knew I was late. I texted my dad and told him not to hold dinner. Then I walked with a spring in my step through the barn toward the road.

Madeline's mother's car was still in the parking lot. What were they doing? Having a heart-to-heart conversation in the freezing cold? I thought she said they had to get going. I was about to go back in the barn so I didn't have to go by the car when I heard Becky.

"You need a ride?" she called out.

Awkward.

The fact was I could use a ride down the dirt road to the bus stop. "Sure," I said.

As soon as I got in the car, I felt the tension. It was like a toxic gas. I got in the backseat beside Madeline and said, "I just need a ride to the bus."

Madeline's mother nodded and looked at me through her rearview mirror. I tried to smile. This could be a long five minutes to my bus stop. "It's nice of you to come out and help with the horses," she said.

"I enjoy it. I'm glad Madeline asked me."

At least she was now driving forward. "This Best Buddies program seems positive for her," she said, still looking at me in her rearview mirror.

Awkward again. We were talking about Madeline in the third person. At least Becky was staying silent and not playing the flirt card.

"We have a really good event coming up," I said. "Did you mention it to your mom, Madeline?"

"The Eveeening of Frieeendshiiip," said Madeline.

"Oh, that sounds like fun," said her mother. "I will have to read the note again."

"I think it will be really awesome." I was sounding stiff, like cardboard. Becky looked out the window and I could see her trying not to laugh.

"Where is your stop?" Her mother asked.

"Um, if you go right at the turn, it's just down a few blocks. But I can walk from the turn."

"It's fine," she said. "I can drive you."

No one said anything for the rest of the drive, which was no more than two minutes but felt like hours. Finally, we were at the bus stop.

"Thank you again for the ride," I said.

"If you were nice," said Becky to her mom, "you would drive him *all the way* home."

"No. No." I opened the door. "I'm good, really. I catch the bus all the time." I popped out of the car and said one more quick thanks before I shut the door. I saw the bus coming and made a run for it.

CHAPTER NINE
MADELINE

"He seems nice," said my mother after we dropped Justin off at the bus stop. "Remind me again about this event. The one he was talking about."

"It's wiiith anooother school," I said. "At a commuuunity ceeentre. On a Friiiday niiight."

"It's not like a date, is it? I think he's too old for you."

"Jeez, Mom," said Becky. "Are you serious? It's the Best Buddies club not Match.com or *Tinder*."

"How do you know about those?" She glared at Becky. "Is your father on those sites?"

"Relax. I watch television." She put her feet on the front dash. This always bugged my mother. After their fight in the parking lot about Becky's piano lessons and her schoolwork and her friends, this was just one more of Becky's plays to get under Mom's skin. Same as when Becky refused to let Mom meet her new friends or even tell her their names.

"It's nooot a daaate," I said from the back seat.

This time my mom glanced at me in her rearview mirror. "I think this could be a nice event for you," she said. "Becky, I would like you to go with Madeline. I could take you girls shopping and buy you each a new outfit for the night. It's such a positive club. Becky, have you ever thought of joining?"

"I caaan go byyy myyyself." Best Buddies was my thing, not Becky's.

"It might be a nice night for the two of you." My mom wasn't giving up. I wished she would. My head was starting to pound.

"I don't want to go to *that*," said Becky. "It'll be lame."

She'd rather hang out in the park, I thought, *smoking with her new friends.* More head pounding.

"Iiit's nooot laaame," I muttered. I pressed my fingers to my temples to stop the throbbing.

"Okay, so it might not be lame," said Becky, "but, for me—note I said *for me*—it wouldn't exactly be fun." Becky slouched further in her seat.

"I think you could try harder to like this group," said my mother.

In the back seat, anger bubbled beneath my skin. Why did they have to fight all the time? They kept nattering. Back and forth. As I listened, and tried not to listen, everything inside me was bubbling and boiling.

Suddenly it hit me. And it just overflowed. I started kicking the back of Becky's seat with my feet. I kicked and kicked.

"Go, Maddie, go!" Becky cheered me on. My feet were kicking her back. She was bouncing in the front seat and laughing.

My mother swerved to the side of the road. "Breathe, okay, Madeline? Just breathe."

"Yeah, Maddie, breathe," said Becky. "*Mommy* said you should breathe."

"Becky, you are not helping."

Suddenly, my anger vanished, replaced by laughter just below the surface of my skin.

"Yeees, sheee iiis," I said. Sometimes, it's like my pores open up and let out any emotion that's trapped in there. And right then, my pores popped open and I started laughing. And laughing. And Becky laughed along with me.

My mom started driving again. She didn't say a word, but she also didn't laugh along with us.

After a few minutes I calmed down and stopped laughing. This time it was my turn to sigh. I leaned my head back and closed my eyes. It took a lot of effort to make my brain relax. It took effort to make it work and effort to make it slow down.

We got home and I got out of the car and went right to my room.

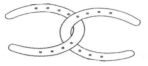

I must have dozed off because I was groggy when I heard the knock on my door. *Where was I? What time was it?*

I sat up. Then I picked up my phone—5:30 already. I'd been sleeping since five. How many minutes?

How many, Madeline? Come on brain, work. Do the math.

Another knock and a little squeak of my door.

I couldn't figure it out. I just couldn't.

"Maddie," said Becky.

"Yeeeah."

She opened the door, walked in, and quickly shut the door behind her. Then she came to my bed and sat down. "I'm sorry I said that about the Best Buddies. It's not lame. It's a great club for you."

"Iiit's ooookay," I said.

"Listen, I have an idea."

I didn't reply. I wasn't sure I was up for her new idea. Anyway, I was still waking up. My brain had to log on.

"Are you okay?"

"I waaas sleeeeping."

"That's good. Your brain does better with rest." She paused. "So…I was thinking. We should go live with Dad."

I frowned. "Daaad?"

"Yeah. I know he doesn't live in our school district but…that Nora kid at school doesn't and neither does Justin."

"Juuustin?" Becky's conversation was making me dizzy. It was jumping around. Nora? Justin? I needed to digest what she said for a few seconds.

As if she understood, Becky just sat beside me for a bit. Finally she asked, "Can we continue?"

I nodded.

"Justin got kicked out of his last school you know. That's why he's at ours. He got in a fight with the kids who bullied his sister."

"Faaaith," I said. "I've seen phoootos of heeer."

"Whatever. This isn't about her. It's about us, and moving to Dad's. Because of your accident, I'm sure we could both stay at our high school even if we moved to Dad's. We can just say it's for your mental health or something like that. Of course, he'd have to drive us to school sometimes or we could catch the bus. It's just one transfer."

"Whaaat about Mooom?"

"Mom? She doesn't let us do anything. Especially you. She grounded me for coming in at like 8:00 o'clock. I'm doing this as much for you as me, you know. Dad would let me quit piano—well, he doesn't even have a piano—and wouldn't ask a zillion questions about my friends."

"I dooon't knooow," I said. And I didn't. It was too much information and too many decisions for me to organize today. I was tired.

"I don't want to push you, but this would be best for you. For both of us."

I thought about my dad and how he travelled for his work. "Daaad isn't alwaaays hooome," I said.

Becky stood up and grinned. "So? That's the best part!"

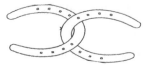

None of us talked much at dinner. My mother tried but I just couldn't.

I had to concentrate on putting food in my mouth and chewing. After dishes were done, she asked me about my speech therapy.

"Nooot toniiight," I said. "Tomooorroow."

"Madeline, you need to work on this," she said.

"Nooo. I'm tiiired."

"If you don't work on it you won't get better. I had a chat with your speech therapist and she doesn't think you're doing the work."

"Leeeave meee aloooone."

I left the kitchen to go up to my room and Becky followed me, even though Mom had already told her she needed to practise her piano. Of course they'd had another fight about it.

"We have to live with Dad," she said. "Mom is making us both crazy. She goes on and on about piano with me and with you it's your speech therapy."

I didn't answer and kept walking up the stairs, holding onto the railing for balance.

I couldn't imagine not living in this house. And what about *Mom*? Sure, she nagged but she was Mom. She would miss us too. I thought about Justin's mother and how he said she missed his sister every single day. Granted she had died and we were still alive. But still.

Becky and I both went to our own rooms. I sat on my bed and stared at the wall for a few minutes. Too many things were spinning in my mind.

I picked up my computer. I opened it to the poem I had written about the Best Buddies. It had taken me weeks to get the words right.

Hair, size, eyes, feet, brains, ideas, thoughts, movement.
Define us.
No two people are alike, not even if from the same egg.
Some can walk, some can talk, some can run fast.
Some can't do any of that.

Some can sing, some can add and subtract, some can explain the stars.
Some can't do any of that.
Some recite bones, some like to cook, some squeal in excitement.
Some don't do any of that.
Who likes ice cream? I don't, you say.
I do, you say.
I can't, you say, it makes me sick.
Who says we have to be the same?
Magazines, television.
Who cares what they say?
I am me. You are you.
We can all be Best Buddies, be us, be friends.
Respect
what we can and cannot do.
Learn
from each other.

I could hear Becky playing the piano downstairs. She really was good. Her fingers flew across the keys. I read my poem one more time. Then I thought about what Justin had said, how he wanted to read it. Could I also be good at something?

So I sent it to him.

He sent me a message back right away.

This is amazing!!!!!

I laughed at all the exclamation marks.

Thx, I wrote back.

I have an idea about this poem. I will talk to you in the morning.

I wondered what he meant.

At around nine, I dressed in my pajamas, washed my face, brushed my teeth, then I went downstairs. The piano playing had stopped. My mother was reading the newspaper in her favourite chair in our family room, her legs tucked up under her, a cup of tea beside her reading lamp.

"I'm goooing to beeed," I said.

She put down her paper. "Are you okay?"

"I praaactised," I said.

"That's good. I know it's hard for you but it's really important."

"I knooow."

"It will help you later in life."

"Iii'm tiiired."

"That's a big step for you," she said. "Knowing when you're tired."

I nodded. She was right. If I knew when I was tired and got some rest I wouldn't have so many emotional outbursts. The psychologist told me that.

"Gooood niiight," I said.

"Good night. I love you."

"I looove you toooo."

"Becky already came down and said good night. When you go back up, tell her I love her too, because I really do. You girls are my whole life."

I went back upstairs and knocked on Becky's door. When she didn't answer, I peeked in and saw a lump under her bed. I had to tell her what Mom said. But when I went to the bed, she wasn't there. She'd put all her stuffed animals in her bed to make it look like her. She must have sneaked out after she said goodnight to Mom.

Back in my room, I turned off my light and lay still. A move to Dad's would be weird. I'd lived in this house my entire life. People seemed to be pushing me in all directions. Becky's idea of moving to Dad's was for the wrong reasons. I closed my eyes. I couldn't think about it all now.

I awoke in the middle of the night and felt an arm around me. Becky was in my bed, curled up beside me, her hair falling on my shoulder. I pulled her arm closer to me and fell back asleep.

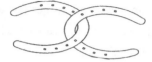

A car swerved to a stop in front of me and Becky as we stood at the bus stop. The morning had gone okay, and Becky had got ready for school without any fuss. I didn't ask her what time she got in or where she'd gone.

"Get in!" Cassandra yelled from the car.

Becky grabbed my hand. "We got a ride, Maddie. We don't have to catch the bus with Mr. Grump." The bus driver had given us a lecture after another smoking incident and said the next time there was trouble, we were off the bus. Forever. Three strikes you're out, that's what he'd said.

"Iii'll caaatch the buuus," I said.

"Come on. A ride is way better."

I allowed myself to be pulled to the car. Why? I'm not really sure. But I did. Becky pushed me into the back seat and sat beside me.

Cassandra was in the front seat. An older girl was driving and I think I recognized her, or had seen her in the halls. I think she was Cassandra's older sister. She drove fast and I thought I might be sick in the back seat. Then she pulled over to the side. And there was Molly and Gwinnie. They pushed their way into the back seat with me and I pushed myself right over, until I was almost hugging the car door. They were laughing about something.

"You owe me, Cassandra," said the older girl driving. "Picking everyone up."

"Yeah, I know," said Cassandra.

The older girl peeled away from the curb. Being squished in the car was making me uncomfortable. It was like I couldn't breathe. How close were we to the school? I looked out the window, trying to get my bearings. Where were we? Could I walk? I didn't even care if I was late. I could feel everything inside of me bubbling, ready to explode. I was going to lose it soon if I didn't get out of the car. I counted to ten. No good. Didn't work. I tried to breathe. No good either. Made me almost hyperventilate.

"I...haaave to geeet ooout," I said.

"Chill," said Cassandra. "We're almost there."

Becky turned to look at me. "Relax, Maddie, okay? We're almost at the school."

"I caaan't," I gasped. "Leeet meee ooout."

"Two minutes," said Becky.

I tried so hard to breathe.

"It's okay, Maddie."

It wasn't okay. I wasn't okay. And then it erupted. Well, I erupted like a hot lava volcano. "Leeet! Meee! Ooout!"

"Holy crap," said Cassandra. "Now that's a set of lungs."

Gwinnie laughed. "That pierced my ears."

"What kind of friends you got, Cassandra?" The older girl drove even faster.

"Stop the car," said Becky. "We have to get out."

"Never again, Cassandra," said the older girl. She yanked the steering wheel and swerved over to the side of the road. I struggled with the door, trying to open it. Trying. Trying.

"Get out of my car," said the older girl.

"Becky, get her out of here," said Cassandra.

Finally, I got the door open and almost fell out. I didn't care if Becky came with me. In fact, I didn't want her to. I stumbled but managed to right myself and throw my backpack on my back.

Becky got out. "I'll meet you at school," she said to her friends and slammed the car door. The car sped away, the noise deafening.

"We were almost there!"

"I diiidn't waaant a riiide!"

"It beats catching the bus."

"Nooo!"

"You are so hard to get along with."

"Sooo aaare yooou." My brain was clicking with so many words, but they weren't moving fast enough to my mouth. I wanted to tell her that I was fine, that I could do my own thing and she could do hers. I didn't want to be friends with her friends. I had my own friends. No words came out.

I stomped away from her.

"Maddie, wait up."

I kept walking but, of course, she caught up with me. "I'll go in with you."

I stopped walking and turned to her. "Nooo."

She frowned. "Why?"

"You juuust…waaant a laaate…sliiip."

"That's not true."

"Yeees. It iiis." I could feel tears under my eyelids. If I started crying I might not stop. Then I would have to endure the laughs and stares of girls in the restroom at school when I tried to fix my blotched skin.

"I'm sorry," she said. "I'm so sorry." Then…she started crying. I stopped walking and stared at her for a few seconds. Becky crying? At school?

"Everything is my fault," she mumbled.

I stepped forward and hugged her, and she didn't push me away.

"I really am sorry," she said.

"Yooou caaan be frieeends wiiith theeem," I said.

"Never mind. You just don't understand."

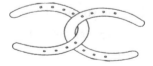

I was late and Mr. Singh was at my locker. Becky had immediately gone to the restroom.

"Sooorry," I said.

"What happened?"

I didn't answer. I opened up my locker and looked at my schedule. Math. Great. Today was just getting worse. Now I had to go look at numbers that didn't make sense. Fortunately, Mr. Singh didn't ask me any more questions. We walked to math together.

But nothing got any better. Gloria kept bugging me about Justin.

"Is he your boyfriend?" she asked for the third time.

"Mr. Siiingh," I said. "I haaave to gooo."

"Okay, let's find a quiet place in the hall."

We went out into the hall and I sat down on the floor. He didn't say anything to me, which was good. Someone talking to me would muddle my brain. It just needed some rest. I sat in the same spot until the bell rang then I stood up and brushed off my pants.

"Are you okay to go to science?" he asked.

"Yeees," I said.

In science, we had to work with partners. The teacher was pairing us up. I lowered my head, detesting this part of school. When I heard my name called, I looked up and saw that I was paired with a girl named Emily. She looked nice but looks were deceiving, except with Becky's friends. They looked like trouble.

"Should we get started?" she asked.

I nodded.

We worked our way through the experiment and I listened closely when she talked to me. Once I had to put up my hand and Mr. Singh came over to explain something that I just couldn't get. Another time Mr. Singh came over without my asking, but I told him I was fine. Emily helped me by reading the text out loud. At the end of class, Emily smiled at me. "We did great work."

"Thaaanks," I said.

She smiled again. "No. Thank you. I'm glad we were partners. Are you in the Best Buddies group?"

I nodded.

"I'd really like to join that."

"I caaan teeell Juuustin for youuu," I said.

"Would you? That would be awesome."

As I walked to the gymnasium to meet up with the Best Buddies for another game time, I ran into Justin. I was finally feeling better about my morning. A game of dodgeball would be fun and I wanted to be with my Best Buddies group.

"I'll walk with you," he said.

I nodded. Then I thought about Emily. I smiled. I had remembered. "A giiirl from…my sciiience class…waaants to beee a Beeest Buuuddy."

"Fantastic," he said. "Invite her to our Evening of Friendship event."

"Okaaaay."

He held up his hand for a high-five. "Good recruiting," he said. Then he grinned at me. "So…I was thinking about your poem."

"Yoooou liiiked iiit?"

"Liked it? I loved it! I didn't know you could write like that."

"I uuuse a cooomputer. I caaan't wriiite by haaand."

"Who cares what you use to write? It's really good. Now…I have an idea. How would you like to read it out loud at the Evening of Friendship event?"

Me. Read aloud. Sure, I had to read aloud in speech therapy but this would be different. I would have to read to a room full of people. "Cooould you reeead it fooor me?" I asked.

"I could. But it would mean so much more if you read it. Think about it," he said.

CHAPTER TEN
JUSTIN

"**H**ow'd you like the movie?" Anna asked as we left the movie theatre.

Light snow fell from the inky night sky. Winter was still here but not for much longer. The snow made me think of the sleighs and the horses.

Anna had picked me up and we'd gone to see a comedy; light laughter, stupid dialogue. Friday night. Something to do. Easy.

She nudged me. "Earth to Justin."

"Sorry," I said, shaking my head. "It was good." I swung her hand. "I needed something funny. And the popcorn was great."

She laughed. "I thought it was good too. Movie and popcorn. And ditto on needing something light. Way too much studying this week."

I wanted to say *me too* but that would have been a lie. My homework had gotten done but I had accomplished little extra to boost those marks. At least I had gone online and looked at applications for the local college. Nothing more than that though. I didn't even know what I wanted to take.

"You want to get together and study tomorrow morning?" she asked.

"I'm going out to the horses," I said. "Maybe in the afternoon."

"Okay."

I lifted my face to the sky, allowing the light snowflakes to dampen my skin. "With this snow we might get to take the sleighs out again. The kids loved them."

"Yeah, it was special," said Anna. "Those little horses are adorable. I've never been much of a horse girl but I liked those teeny tiny ones."

We walked silently for a few seconds. Then she said, "So I've made my decision."

"About what?"

"Next year."

"And?" I'm not sure I wanted to talk about this. Next year seemed far off but close too. I wished I had some idea what to do.

"I'm going to California," she stated. "I got in. I heard the other day. My mom and I talked and she said she'd saved enough for me to go where I want to go. And I really want to get into Stanford for medical school. I think this is my best bet."

"California, eh? That's a long ways away. But good weather." *Why would I say that?* "Um, I guess I should say congrats. Way to go for your dreams."

"You need a dream too." Still holding my hand, she gently swung my arm.

My shoulders sagged and I stared at the ground. I dropped her hand and shoved both of mine in my pockets. "Sometimes I feel so lost." I sighed before I straightened my shoulders and stopped walking. She stopped too and faced me. I reached down and touched her cheek. "But this isn't about me tonight. I really mean it when I say congrats."

"Thanks." She stood on her tip toes and kissed me. The snow kept landing on both of us, almost as if they were wrapping a cocoon over us. I put my arms around her, and she rested her cheek on my chest. "Say you'll visit me."

"I'll visit you," I said.

But deep down I wondered if I really would.

Anna pulled up in front of my house. I turned to her and touched her face.

She leaned her cheek into my hand. Sometimes the simplest gestures were the strongest. I saw her chest rising and falling.

"See you tomorrow?" She smiled at me.

"Yeah," I said quietly.

I leaned over and took her in my arms and kissed her, and kissed her, and kissed her, almost as if I wanted to hold onto her and not let go.

When we broke apart, I could see the tears on her face, glistening from the streetlight. She stroked my cheek. "It's going to be hard to say goodbye."

"Let's just enjoy now," I said. I nuzzled her nose with mine.

"Agreed," she said.

I got out of the car and stood on the front sidewalk, watching her drive away. When the red lights of her car were out of sight, I looked up at my house and noticed the upstairs bedrooms were dark, but there was a light on downstairs.

Inside, my mom was up and sitting at the kitchen table.

"Mom," I said. I glanced around. "Where's Dad?"

"He just went up to bed. I said I'd be up in a few minutes." She stood and moved toward the sink. "Was the movie good?" She turned on the faucet.

"Yeah. It was a comedy."

"That's good." She turned to look at me, sipping her water. "How's Anna?"

"Good. She's going to California next year. She made up her mind."

She tilted her head a little and looked me right in the eyes. "Are you going to be okay with that?"

I shrugged. "I have to be," I said. My mom didn't need to hear about my sorry life. I forced a smile. "Are you still coming to see the miniature horses tomorrow?"

She nodded. "I think so."

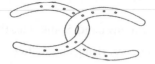

Once my mom had gone upstairs, I looked in the fridge. Then I looked in the pantry. Nothing. Like, nothing *good*. I checked the time. It was only eleven and I was still wide awake. A walk would feel good. And so would snacks.

With my hands shoved deep in my pockets, I walked the five blocks to the corner store. I kept looking up, for stars, but the snow clouds were too thick.

Faith. Are you there?

I approached the store and saw a group of kids hanging around the front. Normal. There were always kids here, and the truth was, I was never one of them. I was considered a bad boy and kicked out of my school because I had beaten the crap out of a kid who had bullied my sister. But I'd never hung around convenience stores.

I had my head down when I heard the voice. "Justin."

I looked up and saw Becky. She was with those girls she hung around with at school. "Hi, Becky," I said.

"What are you doing out so late?" She giggled as if this was some huge joke.

I eyed her closely but she didn't seem drunk. "I could ask you the same thing," I replied.

"Oh, just hanging with my pals, Gwinnie and Cassandra. Have you guys ever met?"

Both girls puckered their lips and made loud kissing sounds.

I shook my head and moved toward the door of the store. I would get what I needed and leave.

"You're such a bore," said Becky.

One of the girls, either Gwinnie or Cassandra, pulled at Becky's jacket. "Come on, let's get out of here," she said. "He *is* boring."

I couldn't stand much more so I pushed by them and entered the store. I saw them walking away as the cashier rang up my bill.

On the walk home, eating Doritos, I took a detour.

The cold air and snow felt good; I wanted to be numbed. Street lights shone on the fresh snow. Lights from houses made me think that other homes looked happier than mine. I wandered and wandered, up one street, down the next, not even looking at street signs, and then I ended up at my old elementary school. The old playground was still there.

By now I'd polished off the entire bag of Doritos, my fingers coated in fake orange cheese. I made my way to the trash can, tossing the bag into the bin. As I turned to head home, I saw the swings.

My mother used to push me on the swings. Higher and higher. Faith would sit in her stroller. Then when we got older, she would pick me up from school, and Faith would be in the wagon. Then Faith was old enough to go to school herself. That's when the bad times started. Kids said things to her, teased her, tormented her, took her toys that she brought to school for comfort. I tried to protect her but I couldn't be with her every hour of every day.

I brushed the snow off one of the swings and sat down. I sighed. My mother tried too and she protected her like a mother bear. But now I had a mother who didn't even know what I did. Never even knew if I was in the house. I could be out until three a.m. and she wouldn't have a clue. I twisted the swing around.

Don't give up on Mom.

"Faith?" I stared up and saw one star, peeking out from under a cloud. Was that her? Was it really her?

Yeah, I knew it was my imagination but for a moment there, it was good to feel her close to me again.

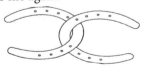

My mother was up in the morning when I got up. She was dressed in the clothes she used to wear to the barn when she went with Faith.

"I'm not sure I should go," she said.

"Mom, they're miniatures. It's really different."

"Of course you should go," said my dad. "Justin really wants you to." He handed my mother her jacket. "It might be cold out there," he said. "I think you should wear this."

"I'm not sure I should go," she said again.

"Just try it once. If you don't want to go again, you don't have to." My dad helped her put her coat on. I watched from a distance. *When had my mother turned into a child?*

"I hope I'm okay," she said. She picked up her pack of cigarettes from the table and shoved them into her jacket.

I looked at Dad. He shrugged. She couldn't smoke at the barn.

With my coffee in a travelling mug, I got in the back seat of the car. The car ride was silent, the air thick and heavy. Not at all pleasant. But it was a car ride. And we were a family, minus one.

When we got to the barn, Mom sat in the car and sat in the car and sat in the car. I didn't move either. I drummed my fingers on my thigh. I fidgeted. Was she going to get out? Should I get out? I waited for her to make a move, the strained minutes ticking by.

Finally, I said, "Um. I better get in there."

"You're going to be fine," said my dad. He touched her cheek. "If you need me, call."

I was actually surprised when she did get out.

"Thanks, Dad," I said.

"I'll pick you up at one."

Mom and I walked toward the barn. "Like Dad said, you'll be fine," I said. "I'm here. Just let me know if you need to get away from everything, okay?"

She sucked in a deep breath and exhaled. "What if I need a smoke?"

"Just go outside and down the road a bit. It's probably not a good idea to light up in the barn or anywhere near the horses."

I think I saw an inkling of a smile creep into her face. "Justin, I do know a little bit about barns."

"That you do," I said.

We entered the barn and headed directly outside. All the horses were already out. Madeline was where she usually was, with Willow. "There's Madeline," I said. "Remember I told you about her."

"Oh my goodness," said my mother. "They *are* little."

We walked over to Willow and Madeline. "Madeline," I said. "I want you to meet my mom."

Madeline turned and smiled. "Hiii."

"Hi, Madeline," said my mother. "My name is Lori. What's the horse's name?"

"Wiiillow."

My mother squatted right down and Willow moved in, nuzzling her nose into her chest. Then I heard a sound I hadn't heard in...I don't know how long. The tinkling of my mother's laugh.

"She's frieeendly," said Madeline.

My mother looked Willow in the eyes. "Willow, you're beautiful." She stroked her nose. "Did you know that your name is special? Real willow branches can bend so they don't get broken. They're different than a lot of the other tree branches. I had a willow tree in my front yard when I was a girl. The more leaves, the more the branches bent. It was a special tree. And you're a special girl." She glanced at me. "Justin did you bring an apple?"

Shocked at how much she had said to the horse, I stammered, "N-n-no, I didn't."

"I diiid," said Madeline. She dug in her pocket for a plastic bag of apple slices and carrots. "She liiikes caaarrots too."

"Thank you," said my mother. "I'll remember for next time."

Next time. I swear my heart skipped like a million beats.

She was feeding Willow when Daphne came up to her and nudged her. Again, my mother laughed.

"Sheee's the baaaby," said Madeline. "She *reeeally* liiikes atteeention." Madeline pointed to Cher. "Thaaat's her mooom. And ooover theeere is Cooowboy."

I stared at Madeline. I don't think I'd ever heard her say so many sentences at one time.

After my mom had petted Daphne, I introduced her to Tonya. Madeline led Willow out to the ring. Once again, the sleighs were out and the horses were getting rigged up to pull the kids around.

Tonya asked my mother if she wanted to help Madeline lead Willow around. She was going to pull one of the small sleighs.

"What would you like me to do?" I asked.

"Help me get the bridles on. And organize the sleighs." She looked at me and grimaced. "And I could really use help cleaning a few of the stalls. Madeline doesn't have time today. We have lots of kids coming."

"Sure," I said.

"You're like Mr. Angel." She patted me on the shoulder. "I'm glad your mom came."

"So am I."

"Madeline seems happy to be helping her."

I glanced over and watched for a few seconds. My mother was talking, actually conversing with someone besides my dad and myself. She'd avoided people for so long, ever since Faith had died, with the exception of appointments and the odd friend dropping by. But even they had stopped coming, after being turned away at the door so many times.

My body felt lighter, my heart more buoyant as I moved inside to clean the stalls.

The morning was all but over, and I'd finished everything Tonya had asked me to do, when I noticed that Becky wasn't around. Madeline was putting Willow away so I asked her, "Where's Becky?"

"She haaad a sleepooover last niiight."

"Oh. With who?" Normally, I wouldn't ask such a nosy question. It wasn't the way I rolled. But after last night I was curious.

"Saaarah. I waaasn't iiinviiited." She shrugged. "I diiidn't waaant to gooo anywaaay."

Yeah, right. Becky was not with anyone named Sarah last night. I wasn't sure what to do with this information. It wasn't in me to tell on Becky but I didn't like that Madeline thought she wasn't invited. From the look on her face, it obviously stung a bit.

"Um, Madeline, I'm not sure Becky was at Sarah's last night. I…I saw her at the convenience store with some other friends."

"Caaassandra?"

I nodded. "And some other girl named Gwinnie."

Madeline didn't say anything in response.

"I shouldn't have said anything," I said.

"It's oookay," she said.

My mother approached Madeline and me. She had stayed outside to talk to Tonya for a few minutes.

"So what'd you think?" I asked, trying to sound like I hadn't just been the biggest mouthpiece of all.

"Faith would have loved it," said my mother.

"Um, yeah," I said, surprised that she had mentioned Faith like that. "She would have."

Then my mother reached for me, wrapping her arms around me and hugging me close. She hadn't hugged me in so long. I melted into her arms and suddenly felt hot, stinging tears behind my eyes. Not here. Not now.

"I'm so lucky to have you," she whispered in my ear.

We pulled apart and I pretended to wipe some dust off my shoe, which was ridiculous because I was in a barn. I heard my mother say to Madeline. "It was such a pleasure to meet you. You have such a way with horses. Thank you for taking me around with Willow."

"Niiice to meeeet yooou too," said Madeline.

I had successfully stopped my tears, so I stood up. "I guess we'll see you on Monday, Madeline."

"Are yooou coming Weeednesdaaay?" she asked my mother.

"I think I'd like that."

Madeline smiled at her. "I'm glaaad you liiike the hooorses."

CHAPTER ELEVEN
MADELINE

"**Y**ou weeeren't with Saaarah last niiight?" I confronted Becky in her room. She was under her covers, sleeping, when she was supposed to be studying or at the very least practising her piano.

"I was so."

"Yooou weeere nooot."

"Why would you even care?" She pulled her covers up over her head. "Mom believed me and we didn't fight about it, so it's fine." Now her voice sounded muffled.

"Yooou liiied to heeer." I walked over to her bed and pulled her covers off her head.

"So?" She frowned at me. "Someone has to. It's like prison in this house. Sit down, okay? I hate you hovering over me like that."

I sat on the end of her bed. "You're goooing to geeet into troooouble," I said.

"Trouble is better than being in jail. Anyway, maybe it's a part of my plan. If I get in trouble, I can plead our case that we need to go live with Dad. That life is unbearable in this house. We need a change. I will straighten up if I get to move and blah, blah, blah."

"It's nooot soooo baaad."

Becky sat up. "How can you say that? I'm doing this as much for you as I am for me. Dad will let you live."

"Mooom triiies."

"Yeah, she *tries* to ruin our lives."

"Whaaat if I waaant to stay heeere?"

"Maddie, come on. We have to stick together." She held up her pinky finger. "Besties."

I shook my head.

"Are you kidding me? Why not? Come on Maddie, please."

I didn't talk because what I wanted to say would make us fight and I could already feel pounding in my head.

Emotions were also bubbling. I had to get out of Becky's room. I went to stand up but she grabbed me by the shoulders. "You have to do this."

Pounding. Pounding. Right against my skull. It was going to happen. "Leeet meee gooo!"

"Don't freak out. Please."

Too much. Too much. The pounding hurt. Emotions were coming at me, hard. Why couldn't I control them? I started hitting my head. *Thwack. Thwack. Thwack.*

Then I felt the arms around me. "Maddie, stop, okay?" Becky spoke softly. She held me tight. Tender. Gentle. "I'm so sorry. I'm really sorry." She took my hand and kissed my knuckles.

And just like that, the emotions that had arrived in seconds, left me in seconds. She had this over me. She did. And I hated that she did. Although I liked that she did too because she was the only one who could stop the stupid lathers.

"See?" she said. "You need me. We have to stay together."

I left her room and crawled into my own bed, ducking my head under the covers.

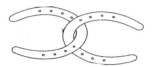

"Hey, something the matter?" Justin asked me on Monday. He had brought the game, Mexican Train, and I was trying to listen to the rules, but it was too much for me, too many rules, and all the words about the rules were bouncing. We had played Dominos and this was a similar game but there seemed to be more things to remember.

"We don't have to play," he said.

"Nooo. I'd liiike to. It heeelps." I put my tiles on the wooden holder. I tried to figure out the colour schemes, numbers. But I couldn't.

We started playing again, but I just couldn't concentrate, and I made mistakes. I didn't count right or add or make the right path. Justin did try to help, he really did, but I was just stupid. *Stupid.*

"Let's pack it up for today," he said.

I nodded. Tears prickled behind my eyes.

"Hey, it's okay," he said. He put my tiles in the box. "My mom is coming again on Wednesday night."

Immediately, my emotions relaxed, just like they always did with Becky. "Sheee's niiice," I said.

"I'm glad you liked her. She really liked you." He smiled at me. "She's not perfect but she's my mom."

"I geeet thaaat," I said. And I did. Had she really liked me?

"Have you thought any more about reading your poem? We talked to the Best Buddies people from the other school and they thought it was a great idea. Of course, I didn't let them read it." He winked at me. "I didn't even let Anna read it. I want it to be a surprise for everyone."

"I triiied to praaactise," I said.

"That's good. Practice is good. "

"Whaaat if nooo ooone undeeerstaaands meee?"

"We will all understand you. Just talk slowly. Don't try to rush. I'll listen to you if you want to practise with me."

"Oookay," I said.

Justin and I just talked for the rest of the period about school and the Best Buddies event and he even asked me to give him suggestions about different events for our group. I suggested another dance because the first one had been so much fun, and now everyone in the club knew each other better. The bell rang and I picked up my backpack.

"What do you have next?" he asked.

"Sciiience."

"I can walk with you."

I nodded. "Mr. Siiighn is meetiiing me theeere. Wheeere's Aaanna?" I asked.

"She had to tutor during lunch."

"Sheee's sooo smaaart."

"Yeah. She'll make a good doctor one day."

"Whaaat dooo you waaant to be?" I stared up at him as we walked.

He shrugged. "I dunno."

"I dooon't knooow either," I said.

He glanced at me. "You're young," he said. He paused for a second before he said, "I'm in senior year. I'm supposed to know."

We walked the rest of the hallway without talking and, when we came to the roundabout area, he had to go in the opposite direction of me. I hadn't seen Becky all day, but then lately that had been the norm. She'd been skipping a lot.

"Hey, Madeline!" I heard a voice behind me. I stopped and turned to see Emily.

"Hiii," I said.

"You going to class?"

I nodded.

"Can I walk with you?"

"Suuure."

At first Emily chatted about science, which was okay because she did all the talking. But then she asked me a question. "Oh, did you talk to Justin?"

I nodded. "He saaaid to cooome to the Even...ing of Frieeend...shiiip."

"Perfect," she said. "Just let me know the details." She sounded honestly happy.

"Iiit wiiill be fuuun," I said.

"I'm looking forward to it." We were almost at the science-room door. "Thanks, again. I appreciate that you did this for me." She gave me a warm, friendly smile. "Now, let's rock this next science experiment."

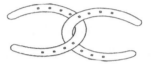

The next fight between Becky and my mom started on Sunday when Becky dyed her hair black. Oh, and gave it purple streaks. I had to agree with my mother; it looked hideous. And they continued nattering at each other, about little things, all the way to Wednesday.

We were in the car on the way to the barn. I sat in the back and looked out the window because I didn't want to look at the back of Becky's head, with her new black hair. Instead of looking alike, we looked opposite. Once again, Becky didn't want to go to the barn, and I didn't care if she did or not but my mother was determined to make her go.

"Whyyy doooes sheee haaave to goo?" I asked.

"Because she signed up to volunteer and she needs to do this. It is important to follow through on commitments. This is a *good* thing to do."

"This is a *good* thing to do," Becky said, mimicking her. She slouched in her seat and pulled out her phone. "It's just because Dad is picking us up and you don't want him near our house. This is the easiest transition for you two scrappers."

"That is not why," stated my mother.

Ping. Ping. Ping.

"Who are you talking to?" Mom asked.

"Friends," snapped Becky.

"Maybe I'll stick around today," said Mom.

"So you can keep an eye on me? And start a fight with Dad when he gets here?"

"Your father and I don't always fight."

I lowered my head. My mom and dad started fighting when I was in the hospital. I would pretend I was sleeping. At that point I couldn't talk so I just tried to block them out of my head. After the accident, they never agreed on anything about me. My mom always wanted to switch my therapists and my dad said to give them a chance. Mom said the doctors didn't know what they were talking about and Dad said to give them a chance.

"Yes, you do," snapped Becky.

Becky's right, I thought.

"Maybe I want to watch Madeline," said Mom. "Or perhaps I want to volunteer as well. Tonya can always use help."

"Juuustin's mooother is coooming," I said from the back seat. The bickering was getting to me and I wanted to change the subject. Plus, Tonya always does need help.

Becky turned around. "You are not making this any easier."

Mom's Bluetooth rang loudly in the car and she pressed the button. It was her boss asking for some document she needed right away. After she hung up she said, "Looks like you're off the hook."

"Maaaybe neeext tiiime," I said. I wouldn't mind having Mom help out at the barn.

My mother looked at me through the rearview mirror. "Thank you for that, Madeline. I will make sure there is a next time."

My mother dropped us off and as soon as she drove away, Becky glared at me. "You're acting like such a suck around Mom."

"I meeeant iiit."

"You're so annoying right now. Don't you get it? We need to get away from her!" Her phone rang and she turned from me. I watched her as she answered it, waving her hands, the black nail polish gleaming in the sun. My sister didn't look like my sister anymore.

I went through the barn and outside to where Justin's mother was already feeding Willow something. I didn't see Justin anywhere but he had to catch the bus from school. He'd told me that at lunch.

"Hiii, Looori," I said.

"Madeline! Hello. How are you?"

"I'm gooood." She had something orange in her hand. "Whaaat are yooou feeding heeer?"

"I cooked up some sweet potato. Faith loved feeding this to the horses. I wanted to see if Willow liked it too." She petted Willow. "And she does." She held up a big freezer bag. "I brought enough for the others too."

I patted Willow too. "Cooowboy eats aaanythiiing," I said.

"Is he the bigger male?"

I nodded.

"Sometimes Faith liked to ride this one male at the barn she went to. He was such a doll. So even tempered. It was almost as if he knew he needed to go slow with her. They're such smart animals."

Willow whinnied so loudly that we both laughed. "Sheee liiiked thaaat," I said.

"I can clean the stalls today," she said.

I looked to the barn door. Still no Becky. "Oookay," I said.

Tonya was getting the sleighs ready when she waved me over to her. Willow walked with her head held high, like a royal lady. All she needed was a crown.

"I'm ready for Willow." Tonya held the bridle up. Willow tapped her foot on the ground and snorted.

"Sheee's reeeady too." I laughed.

"She is." Tonya patted the horse's back. "Willow, baby, this will probably be the last day for the sleighs."

Glancing upward, the sun toasted my skin. Water dripped from the roof of the barn and puddles were forming where there used to be snow. Soon it would be spring. Then summer. Where would I be living then? With Mom? Or with Dad?

I was helping Tonya when I heard a car. The bad muffler sound was too familiar. I glanced over at the parking lot and saw Cassandra and Gwinnie jump out of the car that had picked up Becky and me the other day. Why were they here? Was Becky leaving again? I wish Mom would have stayed. She needed to stay. Dad would be so mad if he showed up and Becky was gone.

But Becky didn't leave. She stayed. And so did her friends. They all walked over to the wooden fence. I could hear them laughing, see them pointing at the horses. Then I saw Gwinnie put a cigarette in her mouth. *Oh no.* I looked to Tonya, hoping she had seen as well. I wanted her to go over and tell her to put it out.

Suddenly, Justin came running up the road. He had told me he'd be late because he didn't have a ride; Anna was busy working on a group project. When he saw Becky and her friends, he went over to them and I knew by his gestures that he was telling them to put out their cigarettes.

"What's going on over there?" Tonya asked.

"Theeey're smoooking," I said.

"Smoking? Hold this bridle for me."

Tonya stomped over but Gwinnie put out her cigarette before she got there. Justin shook his head at them and walked toward the barn. Tonya talked to them for a few minutes, her head bobbing up and down, before she came back to me.

"I'm worried about Becky," she said.

We worked for a few minutes before Justin slid the barn door open and walked down the ramp with the wheelbarrow. His mother walked behind him. They both went over and dumped the manure before they came over to us.

"Sorry I'm late," he said. "My bus was really off-schedule today. What do you need me to do?"

"First off, thanks for getting them to butt out," said Tonya. "So dangerous." She paused. "Justin, why don't you help out with Cowboy again, and Lori you can walk Willow with Madeline." She turned to Lori. "Thanks for cleaning the stalls."

"No problem. I liked doing it." Lori smiled. She turned to Justin. "Willow likes sweet potato."

"Really?" said Justin. "Cool." Then he tilted his head. "Did *you* cook it up for her?"

"I did," said Lori. Then she looked away as if she was embarrassed. I wondered why.

Lori and I walked Willow around and around. First we took Maala for a ride. Then we took a little boy named Casey, who has autism. His mother really helped with him but he seemed to like the ride. At least that's what his mother said. She kept saying, "I'm so happy. He likes this."

Every time we walked by Becky and her friends I glanced over. She gave me little waves. I guess big ones would have been embarrassing? But she didn't look like she was trying to leave like the last time her friends had shown up.

I liked being with Lori. Every once in a while she said something about it being a beautiful day or she liked feeling the sun on her face, or she pointed out to me how Casey looked happy, but she didn't grill me or make my head hurt thinking of how to answer questions.

On our third walk around with Casey, Becky and her friends were gone. Dad was going to be furious. If she wanted to live with Dad, leaving the barn when he was picking us up was such a dumb thing to do.

"Don't worry," whispered Lori. "I think your father is here and your sister is with him."

I looked over and I did see my dad's car. I also saw Tonya wave at us, gesturing for us to bring Willow in.

"Thanks so much," said Tonya when we were by her. "And again, you did an amazing job cleaning the stalls."

"Thanks," said Lori, suddenly quiet.

"I'll cleeean theeeir hooves," I said.

Tonya waved her hand. "Don't worry. I got here early and did it before anyone got here."

"Oookay," I said.

I saw Dad and Becky over by the gate. With a big smile on his face, Dad waved at me. Then he carefully opened the gate. I walked Willow over to him because he was still wearing his dress shoes and suit. He bent right down and whispered in Willow's ear, "Are you treating my girl right?"

She snorted.

"Alwaaays," I said.

I heard a car leaving and I knew which car it was by the noise. Dad didn't look over to the parking lot. Becky looked at me and put her finger to her lips. Had Dad even met Becky's friends? Or had they hidden from him?

I introduced Lori to my father but she didn't say too much. Just hello.

"I'll let you finish up and I'll meet you at the car," he said.

Lori and I walked into the barn. "That was fun," she said. "Thanks for allowing me to help with Willow."

"Nooo proooblem." I really liked Justin's mother and I was glad Justin had told me that she liked me too. I think it was hard for her to talk too, but in a different way. We were both happy to be quiet and just walk.

As I went across the length of the barn I noticed the stalls. Tonya was right; all the stalls were spotless.

"Seeee you agaaain," I said to her.

"For sure," she said.

As I was heading over to Dad's car, Becky sidled up to me and linked her arm in mine. "Don't blab about my friends," she whispered.

I didn't say anything.

"Dad doesn't know. And I don't want him to know."

"Whaaateeever." I sighed.

"Don't worry. It's going to be way better at Dad's," she said. "You'll see."

I didn't think I would see because I didn't want things to change.

CHAPTER TWELVE
JUSTIN

I saw them light up, the red spark glowing. I started running.

"Hey, you guys," I said. "Smoking near a barn is just idiotic."

"What are you the cigarette police?" Gwinnie laughed, this shrill, high laugh that grated my nerves. "Like that old guy on the bus. Mr. Grumps."

I glared at Becky. "Are you kidding me?"

She rolled her eyes but she put the cigarette out on the bottom of her heavy-soled boot. Doc Martens. The others followed when they saw Tonya marching over to them.

With dramatic flair, Cassandra held up her Camel cigarette package before she shoved it in her jacket. "All gone."

Tonya shook her head at them and then turned and walked away. I felt for her; she had way too much work to do to be babysitting a bunch of teen girls.

"It would be so fun to ride those little horses," said Gwinnie in a baby voice.

I glared at her. "You would hurt the horse. That's why little kids ride them."

She puckered up her lips. "I wouldn't hurt the little horsy. I could put my feet on the ground and help it walk." She pretended to be on a miniature horse and walk.

Cassandra and Becky laughed hysterically even though it wasn't funny.

"You look like that cave guy on that old cartoon from a million years ago." Cassandra was laughing so much she could hardly talk. "What was his name? The one who used his feet to move his car."

"Fred Flintstone," said Cassandra.

That was enough for me. I'd given them too much of my time already so I left them and went into the barn, thinking maybe one of the stalls needed cleaning since Becky was clearly not helping at all.

I saw my mother before she saw me. Deep in thought, concentration lines etched on her face, she swept the broom back and forth and back and forth, her movement hypnotic almost. She stopped and used a dust pan to pick up the pile she had swept together. For a few seconds, I didn't move. I wanted to watch her move, sweep, bend over, use her body for something besides being in bed.

Finally, I walked toward her. She heard my steps and turned.

"Justin," she said.

"So glad you're here," I said. "Did Dad drive you?"

She nodded. "He took a break from work to bring me over. I think he's gone for his fitness stuff now."

"I'm impressed." I smiled at her and pointed to the stall. "Looks good. I never get it that clean."

"Oh," she said, "I hope I haven't been at it too long." She placed the broom back in its spot. "Maybe we should go outside. I can take the wheelbarrow."

"You did an awesome job, Mom."

"Thanks," she said softly.

"I can take the wheelbarrow for you. I'm sure Tonya needs help."

We walked out to the ring together and Tonya was happy to see us. After I'd dumped the wheelbarrow and put it away, we were given jobs so we split up. As I helped with Cowboy, my favourite horse (because of his mischievous eyes), I kept my eye on Becky and every once in a while

I glanced over to see my mother and Madeline walking around. They seemed content with each other. At ease.

The afternoon skipped along, too fast for me, and soon it was time to put the sleighs away. The sun was dipping, the night air nippy.

"Do you think this is the last day for the sleighs?" I asked Tonya.

"Um, yeah, I think so. But I'll leave them out just in case we can use them again on Saturday. If not, I wouldn't mind a little help on the weekend putting them away in the storage shed. I have a few dads who help too."

"Sure," I said. "I was planning on being here on Saturday anyway."

She threw me a cloth so I could wipe down the bridle. "Your mom seems to be enjoying herself."

"It's been so good for her," I said.

"I'm glad. I hope she keeps coming. She and Madeline seem to get along real well."

"Yeah," I said. I paused for a brief second. Then I asked, "How long have you known Madeline and Becky?"

"Five years or so."

I nodded.

"Madeline's come a long way. There was a time when she couldn't walk. Her progress is unbelievable, really. When she first started coming here, she had to use a walker to get around. And she could barely get one word out."

"She's pretty incredible. I only recently met her."

"You're lucky. She's taught me a thing or two. I'd love to see her work with animals; she's got a gift. Becky's the one who's worrying me right now. She used to be the sweetest kid."

"Sweet?" I couldn't help blurting that out. I found it hard to believe that Becky was ever sweet.

She nodded. "Really sweet, actually. When they first came here, the therapy was about both girls. Their parents were worried about Becky too because they had her going to a psychologist to talk about the accident but she refused to talk. She'd just hide in a corner. Her parents thought horse therapy might help her as much as Madeline."

"Did it?"

"I don't know. Leah never disclosed much to me. Becky hasn't opened up to me either, and now she's heading down a rough path."

"I don't think she's as tough as she acts," I said.

"Definitely not. She's hurting."

In the distance, I heard a car engine and then I saw my dad pulling up in his freshly washed Lincoln. "My dad's here."

"We're done."

"See you Saturday." I found my mom and walked out with her.

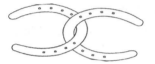

Thursday was the last meeting for our Best Buddies group before the Evening of Friendship event on Friday night. Since I was running the meeting, I hurried down the hall to get to our meeting room so I could be early. We were still doing our fun times in the gym but we had to have a few meetings to make sure the event was organized.

I groaned when I saw Molly and Gwinnie standing right outside the door to the room we used for our meetings.

"The party Friday night is going to be killer." Molly tried to look cool. She had some shirt on that barely covered her and a black leather jacket that had some sort of crest on it. She leaned up against the wall, an unlit cigarette hanging from her mouth.

"We need to score," said Gwinnie. She had her cigarette tucked behind her ear.

"I can steal some of my dad's booze," said Molly.

I pushed past them, hoping they wouldn't see me or wouldn't care that they saw me.

But no go. "Oh look—it's Mr. Cigarette Police," said Gwinnie. She pulled her cigarette out from behind her ear and waved it in front of my face.

I ignored them and headed into the room.

By the time everyone arrived for the meeting, the buzz in the room was deafening but totally electrifying. I couldn't help smiling. Really smiling. Our members didn't get a chance to dress up nice and go out on a Friday night with their friends very often. I stood at the front of the room and held up my hands to get people to stop talking.

"Whoa," I said. "Excited much? Let's talk about the event. All the last-minute details."

"Are we, are we gonna...p-p-lay basketball there?" Don asked.

"I heard that might be one of the games," I said.

"I went shopping with my sister," said Erika, clapping her hands. "I have a new top."

"I'm wearing something pretty too," said Gloria.

"Anna and Muhammad," I said. "Do you want to bring us up to speed on logistics?"

"What are logistics?" Gloria asked.

Harrison answered before I could. "Logistics means the detailed coordination of a complex operation involving many people, facilities, or supplies."

"Thank you for that, Harrison," I said. He rarely spoke but when he did he had something important to say.

I saw Willa lean over and whisper something in Gloria's ear. She nodded as if she understood.

"I managed to get all the permission forms signed and in on time," said Anna. "And I gave them to Mrs. Beddington. Parents are driving and all is good." She held up her hand.

Most everyone cheered, with the exception of Harrison and Erika, who covered her ears.

Next Muhammad stood up. "So, there is definitely going to be music and I guess they have a good variety. Plus, they were trying to rig up a disco ball."

"A disco ball! Like in *Saturday Night Fever*." Erika stood up and did a '70s disco move. "I know some of the songs."

"Me too," said Gloria. "Me too."

I held up my hands again to try and keep the meeting rolling. We only had the room at the school for thirty minutes and many of the parents would arrive at 4:00 to pick them up.

"I am bringing some snacks," said Marcie. And there will be other food as well, punch included. Plus, they are setting up a games table with board games and card games. And I think there are going to be a few other games as well, like 'pin the tail on the donkey' and a fishing game where you can win a prize."

"I played that at the f-f-fair last year." Don threw his arms in the air. "I won a s-s-stuffed elephant."

"I'm not sure the prizes will be that big." Marcie laughed. "But it will be fun to try."

"Should we all go in together?" Anna asked.

"We could," said Marcie. "We could meet in the community centre lobby."

I held up my phone. "Text me if you're going to be late so we don't wait, okay?"

Erika held up her phone. "I can text!"

The meeting ended and the chatter continued about what some were wearing, how there was going to be games, the dancing and, of course, the disco ball. I heard Don ask Marcie if it was something he could play with, like an athletic kind of ball.

After the meeting Madeline came up front to see me. She rarely said anything during the actual meetings. "Myyy frieeend Emiiily is coooming tooomorrow too."

"I'm so glad."

"I thiink she's myyy friiiend," she said, almost shyly.

"We're all your friends," I said.

"I'm neeervous about my poem," she said.

I slapped my forehead. "We didn't practise."

"Iiit's oookay," she said.

"No, it's not. Can you wait just a few minutes for the room to clear? You could read it to me now, if you have it with you."

"I have it on my computer."

"Awesome."

I was putting my notes away in my backpack when Anna asked, "You ready to go?"

I looked up. "Can you wait a few minutes for me? If not, I can catch the bus."

"I can wait. What do you need to do?"

Madeline turned to Anna. "I'm goooing to praaactiiise my poooem. Yooou caaan staaay, toooo."

"Are you sure?" Anna asked. "Justin wanted me to be surprised."

Madeline nodded. "Yooou caaan watch nooow."

The room cleared in five minutes and I closed the door so we could have some privacy.

"Iii'm neeervoooous," said Madeline.

"I understand that," I said. "I'd be nervous too, but that's okay. You're going to be brilliant."

"I once heard if you stare at an audience and think of them in their underwear you won't be nervous," said Anna, laughing. "I think that would just make me laugh and not be able to talk."

Madeline started laughing. "Iiin theeeir uuunderweeear," she said. She shook her head. "I caaan't dooo *thaaat.*"

We all laughed.

Finally, I held up my hands. "We only have a few more minutes," I said.

Madeline nodded. "Oookay, I caaan dooo thiiis."

Anna and I quieted down too. The room was silent, with only the white noise of buzzing fans and rattling windows. Madeline inhaled a big breath then she started to speak. Her words came out slow but clear. Every single one. She meant what she was saying and her words sank deep inside me. I clung to them, and to her passion. I guess she made me think of my own life, and how it didn't matter that I wasn't like every other senior with a plan.

I could be different. I could take time to figure it out.

I glanced at Anna and saw her swiping her eyes.

When Madeline was finished, we both clapped, Anna louder than me.

"That was so amazing!" Anna jumped up and gave Madeline a huge hug.

"I heard every word," I said. "Loud and clear."

"Oh, me too," said Anna, putting her hand on her chest.

Madeline smiled. "Thaaaanks," she said. "Fooor liiistening."

"Oh, we were listening all right," I said.

CHAPTER THIRTEEN
MADELINE

Becky stood at my bedroom door, looking like Becky but in a black costume. So in other words, I could see Becky in her eyes, my inseparable twin. I was rifling through my closet looking for something to wear to the Evening of Friendship. Time had run out and Mom had been too busy to take us shopping. Plus, Becky hadn't really wanted to go. They'd fought about it. So I'd lost out and didn't get a new outfit.

"Do you want me to pick something out for you?" She stood hesitantly at my door, as if she needed me to invite her in. Something was up—but what? She was still talking about the "live with Dad" stuff these days, but I had basically decided to ignore her. So she'd kind of stopped but that made me suspicious.

I kept pushing the hangers, one by one. Green shirt. Yellow shirt. I couldn't figure out what to wear and the stress was gurgling inside me, under my skin. Such a simple decision. But one I couldn't make. *Pick something, Madeline. Pick something. Pick something.*

Sometimes even these simple decisions were too much for me.

I refused to look at her. But I had to say something. I did. Finally, I got the words out. "I dooon't waaant to weeear blaaack."

"That's okay." Then like old times she came into my room. "What about that pink shirt I gave you?"

I eyed her suspiciously. But I only saw the old Becky, before she'd changed and gone to total black, fighting with Mom and hanging out with friends who didn't even act like real friends.

Was she back? Or was I just hoping to see something sincere?

"Maaaybe," I said.

"Let's find it and you can try it on," she said with enthusiasm. She moved right over to me and peered into my closet before she started pushing the hangers.

"Here it is!" She pulled the shirt off the hanger and held it up to me. "It will look good with your hair." Her eyes lit up. "Let's flat iron your hair too. Oh, and I have a pair of jeans I don't wear too much anymore and you can have them."

"O-kaaay," I said.

While Becky ran to her room to get the jeans, I put on the pink top and looked at myself in the mirror. I did like the colour because it was not hot pink but a deep pink, almost a fuchsia, and it made my blonde hair stand out. The shirt had buttons down the front and a collar and sleeves that could be rolled up and held at three-quarter length with little buttons. I hadn't worn it to school yet because it was a bit dressy. Or just dressier than I usually wear to school. Would I look okay when I was on the stage reading my poem?

Becky returned to my room with a pair of jeans in her hands.

"Oh, wow! The shirt looks awesome!" She threw the jeans at me. "Try these."

I put the jeans on and once again stood in front of the mirror. She came to stand beside me.

"You look good, Maddie." She put her arm around me and we looked at each other in the mirror.

For a few seconds I stared at us, shocked at how contrasting we looked. Every photo of us when we were little, before my accident, we were dressed in exactly the same clothes, had the same hair style, even down to the same hair accessories. Mom had labelled every photo on the back with something like Madeline on the right, Becky on the left. Just so later on she could tell us apart. Now we looked like total opposites.

"Dooo you liiike weeeearing just blaaack?" I asked. "Ooor is it juuust tooo beee liiike thooose giiirls?"

She shrugged and walked out of the mirror. But for a second I had seen something in her eyes. Something that told me she wasn't as happy with her newfound friends as she thought she was.

"I dooon't caaare whaaat you weeeear. Thaaanks for coooming tooonight," I said. I hadn't told either her or my mother that I was reading my poem.

"It's okay," said Becky. "I don't mind."

Again, I stared at her. What was going on? "Buuut theeere's that biiig paaarty tooonight," I said. "I heeeard Caaassandraaa and Mooolly taaalking."

She shrugged. Then she looked away.

Was she not invited? Had they kicked her out of their group already? So was that what this was all about?

"Yooou're not goooing?" I asked.

"I don't have a ride," she said.

"Aaare they goooing wiiith Caaassaaandraaa's siiister?"

"Yeah." She paused. "*They* are. And a few other friends. Older girls."

"Diiid theeey leeeave you ooout?"

She shrugged. "I don't wanna talk about it."

Okay, so that was it. She was being nice to me because she had been left out. "Let's do your makeup too," she said. She patted the bed. "Sit down."

An ache jabbed me in the heart. I wasn't really her confidante anymore; she didn't want to talk to me. Was it because of my brain? Or because we were different now? After my accident she always told me we wouldn't change. We would still tell each other everything. We would discuss boys and dates and our first kisses.

I sat down but said, "Nooot too muuuch, okay. And nooo blaaack eeeyeliner."

"No. No. Of course not. I'll do some pastel colours."

Becky went to work on my face and I just sat there, still, so she wouldn't smudge anything. We didn't talk.

Then her phone pinged. She leaped up and snatched it off my desk, where she had left it when she came into my room. Within seconds she fired off a few texts.

"Are yooou fiiinished wiiith my maaakeup?" I asked.

"Give me a sec." She didn't look up from her phone.

"Hooow muuuch looonger?"

"I said give me a sec!"

"Is iiit Mooolly?"

Suddenly, she frowned and I knew she was upset about something. Her lips pursed and she gritted her teeth. "What a…," she muttered.

"Whaaat's the maaatter?" I asked.

She shook her head and smacked her phone down on the desk. "Nothing," she said. Then she turned to me. "Let's finish your makeup."

She finished up in a matter of seconds then grabbed her phone and went back to her room, barely saying anything to me. The old Becky had come and gone. I'd lost her to whoever was on her phone.

I was not in the loop she called her life.

I glanced at myself in the mirror and was pleased. Who cared about her tonight? I was going out and I was going to have fun. And I was going to read in front of everyone. My stomach started churning.

You can do it. You can do it.

I smiled at myself. I looked better than I'd ever looked. Maybe someone would ask me to dance. Someone besides Justin. I picked up my phone and when I looked down to check the time, I saw I had a text. Probably from Justin. But when I looked closer, I saw Emily's name. We had exchanged phone numbers in science class but I never thought she would actually send me a text.

hi Madeline it's Emily looking forward to tonight see u there.

I texted right back.

me too see u there.

Excited for the evening, excited I was going out on a Friday night, I went downstairs as it was almost time to go.

My mother was at the kitchen table, papers spread out in front of her. She looked up from whatever it was she was doing when she heard me come into the room. Her face lit up in a smile. "You look nice, Madeline."

"Thaaanks," I said. "Becky gaaave meee the tooop."

"I'm so sorry we didn't get out shopping. I'm so glad Becky helped you." She tilted her head and really looked at me. "Your hair looks great too. Different."

"Beeecky flaaat iroooned iiit for meee."

"And is that a bit of makeup?"

I looked to the floor. Had we done too much? Gone too far? I didn't wear makeup. Was she going to tell me to go take it off like she did with Becky?

"It looks lovely. You look lovely."

"Thaaanks," I said again. *Tell her about your poem. Tell her about your poem.*

I stood in front of her. Then I blurted out, "I haaave a frieeend coooming tooonight."

"A friend?" She winked at me.

"Nooot a boooy." I laughed.

"Okay."

"Emiiily. Weee're scieeence paaartners."

"That's wonderful, Madeline. I'm really proud of you."

Tell her.

"You know, Madeline, I'm thinking we need a shopping day. Maybe just you and me, if Becky doesn't want to go. That top really suits you and…are those Becky's jeans? The ones she bought last summer with her babysitting money?"

I had forgotten that Becky had saved her money to buy these jeans.

"I thiiink sooo," I said.

"Well, they look good. We should buy you some that are similar." She stacked her papers and stood, running her hand through her hair. "Let's get going. Is Becky ready?"

I shrugged.

Even though Becky had left my room angry, she didn't make a fuss getting into the car. My mom kept stealing glances her way, as if she too wondered what was up with her.

When we got to the community centre, my mother said, "Have fun, girls. I will pick you up at nine."

"Sure thing, Mom," said Becky, getting out of the car.

"Thaaanks fooor the riiide," I said.

The lobby of the community centre was a bustling place and I immediately saw our group. Justin waved and came right over. Anna was already with Harrison and he had dressed up too, in khaki pants and a t-shirt underneath a buttoned shirt. Erika wore a pretty yellow top with jeans and Dan had on jeans and some t-shirt with a sports team logo on it. He also had on his signature baseball hat. Most of the other Best Buddies had worn something they didn't normally wear to school.

"You look fantastic," Justin said to me.

"What about me?" Becky asked.

Justin gave her a glance and said, "You too, Becky."

He turned back to me. "We're still waiting for Gloria and Willa."

I glanced at the group to see if Emily had arrived yet but I couldn't see her. "Aaand Emiiily," I said.

"Oh right. I'm glad she's coming," said Justin.

"Sheeee teeexted meeee and saaaid sheeee waaas."

"Great," said Justin.

Becky turned to look at me, squinting as if she was confused about something. "Who's Emily?"

"A frieeend."

"Where did you meet her?"

"Sciiience."

"Oh." She frowned. "You didn't tell me about her."

"Soooo?" I said. She wouldn't tell me about her friends—why should I tell her about mine?

"Come on," said Justin. "Let's go join the group."

As I mingled with my friends, Becky leaned against the wall, her thumbs moving, sending text after text. Would she stay? Or would she somehow find a way to get to the party? There was a part of me that didn't care, but then there was this part of me that wanted her to stay and listen to my poem. So she could hear me do something important.

Anna came up to me, holding a piece of paper. "We have a little bit of a schedule for tonight. Do you want to start off the evening or end the evening? Your choice."

"Whaaat's beeeetter?" My stomach felt a little sick. And my hands were sweating.

"Depends," said Anna. "The beginning starts us off on the right foot but the end is maybe more dramatic. But, for you, if you go early then you might enjoy your evening more." Palms up, she moved her hands up and down to make it look like a balancing act.

I inhaled. Then blew out the air. "Maaaybe...," I glanced over at Becky. She was still hanging around so maybe she would hear me if I went early rather than at the end of the night. "I woooould liiike to geeet it ooover wiiith," I said.

"Great," said Anna, holding up her thumb. Then she wrote something down on the paper she had in her hand. She put her hand on my back. "For the record, I would have chosen first too." She glanced at Becky. "Are you waiting to talk to your sister?"

I nodded.

"See ya inside, then."

I was just about to go over to Becky when Harrison Henry came up to me. "You look lovely tonight, Madeline."

I smiled at him. "Thaaanks, Haaarriiison," I said.

"That colour of pink in your blouse—my mother said that kind of shirt on a woman is a blouse—can be classified more as rose, but definitely not crimson. It isn't dark enough to be crimson, or even a red." He stared down at my feet. "I am extremely glad you chose to wear flat shoes this evening. I don't like high heels. They are hard on the feet. Did you know there are twenty-six bones in the feet?"

Harrison has high-functioning autism and when he starts talking, he talks a lot, which I like because then I don't have to talk. And sometimes he has meltdowns like me.

"I understand," he continued, "that you have survived a brain injury. I find that quite remarkable. I would ask if it was a frontal lobe injury but you don't have any obvious symptoms of frontal lobe damage."

"It waaas a traaaumatic braaain injuuury," I said.

"Traumatic brain injury is a very complex injury and it has a broad spectrum of symptoms and disabilities. Obviously, your speech has been affected and perhaps your coordination. It is the cerebellum that affects motor coordination and the temporal lobe affects memory and learning."

"Aaand mooood," I said.

"Yes. That is correct. I'm sure you are subject to mood swings, or you have some issues controlling your emotions. Ironically enough, I have the same sort of problems and I don't have brain damage. You are doing remarkably well with your progress." He paused. "I told my mother I thought you were very pretty and she said I should ask you to dance this evening."

My cheeks heated up but it didn't feel like I was going to have a freak out. It actually felt good. "I'll daaance with yooou," I said.

"I prefer fast songs," he said. "With the slow songs we might have to touch each other and that concerns me as I'm not sure if you are carrying any germs."

"Thaaat's oookay, Haaarrison," I said. "I understaaand."

"Thank you," he said. "I very much appreciate that. When it is time, I will ask you to dance."

Just then I heard my name and I turned to see Emily.

"Haaarrison," I said. "Thiiis is my frieeend, Emiiily."

Emily stuck out her hand but Harrison didn't return the gesture. "Germs can be spread from hand shaking," he said.

"Good to know," said Emily.

We talked for a few more minutes and Harrison explained to Emily about how he liked *Grey's Anatomy* and how one episode was about a woman with a brain injury. Then he told Emily that he thought I was doing really well with my brain injury.

She turned to me and smiled. "I think you're amazing."

Once everyone had arrived, Justin led us all into a room at the community centre that was decorated with coloured balloons and streamers. Well, everyone but Becky went in. I didn't care. Music played. Tables were set up with food and board games, just like we had talked about in the meeting. A big black curtain cordoned off the photo booth on the far end of the room. Feathered boas and scarves were draped over a portable mirror. Beside the mirror sat two trunks full of clothes and what I guessed might be other accessories. And, as promised, a disco ball hung from the ceiling.

"Oh, wow," said Emily. "This is cool."

I saw people I didn't know from the other school's Best Buddies program. I wondered if anyone had a brain injury, like me.

Justin came over to me and whispered in my ear. "We are going to start in five minutes. Are you ready?"

I sucked in a deep breath and stood tall. "I thiiink soooo." Now I was so glad I had taken Anna's suggestion to go at the beginning of the evening. I wanted to do this. But my stomach felt sick and my throat was really dry.

"I'll be here to help you if you want it," he said.

"I thiiink I caaan dooo thiiis."

"I *know* you can do this."

"I'm goooing eeearly to geeet it ooover wiiith."

"That's what I would have done."

I glanced around the room for Becky. She still hadn't come in.

"I'll beeee riiight baaack," I said.

Becky was still outside, but now she was talking on her phone, instead of texting, and pacing back and forth.

"Why can't she come get me?" I heard her ask. She was probably talking to Cassandra. "I can squeeze in the back seat. I'll even pay her ten bucks."

"Beeecky," I said.

She held up her finger at me. But I couldn't wait. Justin had said five minutes around two minutes ago.

"Beeecky," I said again.

"Maddie, not now!" She went back to her phone. "Come on. *Pleeeease.*"

She glanced at me then took her phone away from her face. "Look, this is your thing," she whispered, "not mine."

"I'm...I'm goooooing tooo..."

"She's not coming with me," she said into her phone without looking at me. She glanced at me and I could tell by the look in her eyes that she hoped I hadn't heard what she said. But I did.

"There you are," said Justin. He walked over to me. As soon as Becky saw him she turned her back and walked away from us.

"Is she coming to hear you?" he asked.

I shook my head. "Noooo. Aaand I dooon't caaare."

"I'll video it on my phone," said Justin. "Then you can show your mom and dad. I bet you didn't tell them either, did you?"

"Nooo. I sooort of wiiish I diiid."

"That's why I'll record it. Then you will have proof." He put his hand on my shoulder as we walked back into the party room. The music seemed louder; the noise of people talking and laughing had risen. I saw a tall, skinny girl with long black hair standing near the front on a little stage. She was from the other school. When she saw Justin, he waved to her. Someone turned off the music and the room got quiet.

"Attention, everyone," she said in a microphone.

Oh no, I hadn't practised in the microphone. Everyone turned to look at her. *Oh no. Everyone was going to look at me.*

"Welcome to our first ever Evening of Friendship. My name is Suzanne and I'm from St. Frances High School. We are going to have some fun tonight!"

Lots of people clapped. Don and Gloria both whistled. Sam cheered loudly. And Erika cheered even louder.

Suzanne put her hands up to quiet everyone down again. "Before we start the music and dancing, we are going to open the evening with a poetry reading by Madeline. Madeline belongs to the Best Buddies group at Sir Winston Churchill. We think it is so important to share our gifts. Madeline is going to share her gift of writing."

Suddenly the room started cheering. *For me. For me.* My knees started to shake. My heart beat. I could feel my blood flowing through my body.

Justin put his hand on my elbow. "I'll walk up with you," he whispered.

I nodded.

I walked carefully because I didn't want to fall. With my bad balance and my shaking knees I knew that was possible.

Justin helped me, guiding me forward, and when we got to the stage he whispered, "You're going to be great."

I slowly walked up the two steps and went over and stood in front of the microphone. My knees felt like Jell-o. My hands were sweating like crazy. What if my voice wouldn't make any sound, like it did after my accident?

I scanned the crowd but didn't see Becky. Why didn't she get off her phone? Why were her friends more important than me? I started to bubble inside. *Oh no. I couldn't lose it.* I just couldn't.

I let my arms relax by my body. I inhaled and exhaled.

For a few seconds I just stood there. Calming myself down. I went to start and…I realized I'd forgotten to bring the paper with me. I didn't have the poem to read. I tried to remember the first line. I couldn't. What was the first word? My brain wasn't going to cooperate. It wasn't going to let me remember. *I couldn't do this.*

Tears pooled behind my eyes. My heart beat out of control.

Then I saw Justin. He smiled at me, and waved a paper, as he walked toward the stage.

"You forgot this," he said. He came up the two steps to the stage and handed me a piece of paper. I looked down and saw my poem. In big black letters.

"You can do this," he whispered. "Just read it like you did for me."

I nodded.

I stared at the first line. Then I started reading:

Haair, siize, eeyes, feeeet, braaains, ideeeas, thoughts, mooovemeeent.
Deeefine us.
Nooo two peeeople are alike, nooot even if frooom the saaame eeegg.

CHAPTER FOURTEEN
JUSTIN

"Weee caaan all be Beeest Buuuddies, be us, be frieeends.
Reeespect
whaaat we caaan and caaannot do.
Leeearn
frooom each ooother."

Madeline finished reading her poem and the room just exploded with cheers and whistles and applause. I kept my phone held high, taping her beaming up on stage. Then I scanned the crowd so her parents could see her huge success.

Beside me, Anna was wiping her eyes. When she saw my phone focused on her, she waved. "Amazing, Madeline. Just amazing." She wiped another tear and laughed. "Yup, I'm crying."

Suzanne took to the microphone again. "Oh wow! Thank you so much, Madeline. That was amazing."

I turned the video off on my phone when the cheering died down.

Up front, Suzanne said, "We are going to turn the music back on. So enjoy the dancing under the disco ball." She did a little dance move up on stage, wiggling her hips and moving her arms. "Oh, and the photo booth is ready to go. It's gonna be a hoot. Enjoy the food and games and let's have a wonderful Evening of Friendship."

Suzanne helped Madeline get off the stage and I went right over to her. I saw her looking around the room, probably trying to find Becky.

There was no way I was going to let that girl mess things up for Madeline. Not tonight.

"You did such an incredible job," I said. I held up my phone. "And I have every word taped."

Emily hugged Madeline. "That was fabulous," she said.

Anna hugged her too. "Stop making me cry, girl."

Madeline laughed. "Thaaat was fuuun. Weeell, sooort of fuuun. Fuun when it waaas ooover."

Then she looked around the room again, scanning the crowd, and something inside me boiled.

"Should we dance?" I asked her.

"I neeeed to goooo to the waaaashroom first," she said.

"I'll go with you," said Emily.

Before the event had started, I had briefed everyone on where the restrooms were since we were in a new venue. And I told everyone to go with their buddy, or *a* buddy, because it was a big facility.

After they had left, Anna linked her arm in mine. "And to think we met because of the Best Buddies."

I leaned into her, inhaling the fresh flower smell of her hair. "Yeah," I said. "Kind of a cool way to meet."

"I'm going to miss this club next year."

"Me too. You should start one if they don't have one at your university."

She nodded, thoughtfully. "Maybe. I'll check into it."

"Madeline was looking for Becky," I said. "Although I don't feel it is *our* responsibility to babysit her tonight, I think I should see if she's still here."

"I didn't see her in the room," said Anna.

"She was outside in the lobby just before Madeline's poem." I paused. "Talking on her phone. I know she's a pain but I kinda feel for her. Tonya told me she used to be really sweet. When an accident like Madeline's happens it can affect everyone in the family."

"Sort of like your family."

"Yeah, like my family and like me. Look at the trouble I got into after Faith died. Fights. School suspensions. I just couldn't stop myself."

Anna grabbed my hand. "Let's go find her. Ease your conscience."

As we walked toward the exit, Anna said, "Oh, by the way, Harrison talked to me all day about asking Madeline to dance. He even made me role play with him."

"Are you kidding me? Like, what kind of role playing?"

"He made me pretend I was Madeline and he asked her to the dance."

"That's awesome," I said.

At that point, we got to the lobby but I didn't see Becky.

"She's gone." Anna also looked around.

"I'm going to go outside and see if she's there."

Sure enough, shivering in the cold, there stood Becky. She was still texting someone.

"Hey, Becky," I said.

She refused to look at me.

"Madeline's looking for you," I said.

She turned away from me.

"Becky, come on. Talk to me."

"Leave me alone." Her voice sounded strangled.

"Hey, what's wrong?"

"Nothing. Didn't you hear me? Leave me alone."

"She's been crying," Anna whispered to me. "You okay, Becky?"

Becky nodded and straightened her shoulders. "I'm leaving soon."

That's when I saw her face. It was red and puffy, and black was smeared under her eyes.

"Why don't you stay?" I asked. "Madeline would love it if you were here."

"This is Madeline's deal, not mine."

"You said you would come, and everyone is having fun. I bet you and Madeline could get some crazy photos at the photo booth."

"I'm not even in your program. Why should you care?"

"Because Madeline does."

"Madeline is fine."

"Did you hear her read her poem?" I asked.

She jerked her head up and stared at me. "She read a poem? My Maddie?"

"She sure did," said Anna. "It was amazing."

"I have it on my phone if you want to see the video."

Suddenly, a car came squealing into the parking lot. Girls screamed out the window. Unfortunately, I recognized some of them. Well, all of them. Cassandra's sister was in my grade, as was her friend Lucy. They sat in the front seat, and the back seat already had three other girls.

I closed my eyes for a second. This was not good. Nothing about the situation was safe.

"Get in, Becky!" Cassandra leaned her torso out the window. Then she threw her cigarette butt to the ground.

"You can't let her go," whispered Anna. "Not with that group."

"Tell the kid to get in, Cassandra, or I'm leaving."

"Are you coming or not?" Cassandra yelled at Becky. "We drove all this way for you."

"Becky, stay," I said. "Please." For a few seconds, I thought I saw some sort of longing in her eyes, as she stared at my phone with the video of her sister.

"Becky! GET IN!" Cassandra shrieked. "We didn't drive all this way for nothing!"

"I told you she was a bloody baby," said Cassandra's sister. "She's a waste of my time!"

"I've gotta go," said Becky, her voice shaking. "Tell Madeline I'm sorry and I'll make it up to her." She looked at me. "And send me the video, okay? I really want to see it."

"Give me your phone number," said Anna.

Glancing between us and the car, Becky rattled off her number.

"You don't have to go," said Anna.

"You don't understand," said Becky.

I touched her arm but she just yanked it back. "Don't touch me!" Then she jumped in the car. It sped away, tires squealing.

"Ohmygod," said Anna.

"I don't want to tell Madeline," I said. "It could ruin her night."

"Let's go inside and figure this out." Anna linked her arm in mine. "But do send the video to her. She really wanted it."

Michael Jackson's "Thriller" blared from the speakers and a crowd danced under the disco ball. I looked for Madeline and saw her on the dance floor with Harrison. Her body was moving, her feet were shuffling, and the smile on her face was huge. Harrison looked a little like a robot dancing but he also was almost smiling. Almost.

Anna pointed to him. "He did it," she said. "He asked her to dance."

"I'm not saying anything about Becky. It's not fair to her," I said.

"Let's leave it for a bit. Let her have some fun. Look at Erika," said Anna.

She was doing the moonwalk, her signature move. Within seconds, everyone started to try and moonwalk.

"Come on," said Anna. "Let's join in."

The laughter in the room escalated and the moonwalk attempts were hilarious. I tried to forget about everything else and concentrate on trying something different. I sucked at the moonwalk. But then I sucked at dancing—period.

Anna covered her mouth with her hand, giggling.

"You be quiet," I said.

"Okay, okay. I know, you're trying."

The song ended and I stood beside Madeline.

"I was hopeless," I said to her. "Two left feet."

"Thaaat was sooo fuuun." Her eyes shone and her face had a slight flush to it.

"Do you want to try some games?" I asked. "Or the photo booth?"

"Phoooto booooth!"

She turned to Harrison. "Thaaank you fooor daaancing wiiith meee."

He gave her a little bow. "It was my pleasure. I will ask you again later if you like."

She nodded. "Suuure."

We walked over together and Sam and Stuart were there, getting ready. Stuart was helping Sam put on huge black glasses that covered his entire face. They were laughing like crazy.

"Yooou looook hiiilariouuus," said Madeline.

"What are you going to put on?" Sam asked Madeline.

She looked around at everything then pulled down a feather boa, wrapping it around her neck. I went for the cowboy hat and red scarf. When I saw the plastic gold tiara I handed it to Madeline.

She giggled. "Wiiillow iiis the priiincess." She put the tiara back and pulled out red glittery heart glasses, the half ones that are on a stick and used at masquerade balls. She held the heart glasses up to her face.

"Looks good," I said. I winked at her. "Suits you because you have a big heart."

We went behind the black curtain and Stuart and Sam joined us. We saw the countdown then heard the snap. The photo printed immediately and we all laughed when we saw our funny faces. Anna and Harrison were next in line. Anna was using a disinfectant wipe to clean off a pair of black glasses, ones like Anna's that were on a stick but they were black, horn-rimmed ones.

"Look, Harrison," she said. "They don't even have to touch you."

"I think the hats are unsanitary," he said.

"Yeah, but the mask isn't," said Anna.

"You are correct."

"I'll even give you a tissue and you can hold on to it that way."

Harrison turned to Madeline. "Would you like to join us in our photo?"

"Okaaay," she said.

The four of us went behind the black curtain and posed. When the photo printed, Harrison had his eyes completely closed. But Madeline was smiling.

A techno-type song started blaring from the speakers and I glanced over at the dance floor. Now the group was dancing like robots.

"Harrison," said Anna. "It's our turn to give out prizes at the fishing game."

"I caaan heeelp," said Madeline.

As we walked across the floor toward the game, Madeline said, "I wiiish Beeecky woooouldn't haaave leeeft."

"I know. I'm so sorry she did."

"Sheee texted meee," she said. "Sheee waaatched a videooo of meee. Diiid you seeend it tooo her?"

"I did. Is that okay?"

"I seeent it to my Mooom and Daaad. Theeey said Becky seeent it too."

"I'm happy she did that," I said. I was also happy that she was staying in touch with Madeline. At least Madeline knew she'd left so I didn't have to be the one to wreck her evening. I eyed Madeline and she seemed to be having a good time, even without Becky.

Madeline and Harrison handed out prizes and Anna and I stood back and watched.

"They're cute," she said. "I take it you haven't said anything to her about Becky."

"Not exactly. Becky has been texting her so she knows what's up and is handling it just fine so far." Then I leaned into her and whispered, "I think *you're* cute."

She gave me a playful slap but leaned against me. Soon, Stuart and Sam relieved Harrison and Madeline from their fish-pond duty.

A song from the musical *Grease* came on and, once again, we were back on the dance floor. This time we tried jiving. At 8:45 we had planned to do a conga line with a 1-2-3 kick. The music came on and I got behind Madeline. This was a hard one for her to do so I kept saying *one-two-three kick*. The conga line was not the best for sure, and legs were flying at the wrong time, but everyone was kicking and moving and laughing by the end of it.

"Thaaat waaas sooo fuuun." Madeline's cheeks were red from the exercise and it made her face shine, including her eyes. Becky or no Becky, she'd had a good time.

The evening ended with one last song and Harrison asked Madeline to dance again. Stiff as a board, he flailed his arms and legs but there was a smile on her face as well as a little one on his. Anna came up to me.

"Look at Harrison," she said. "He's come so far."

"He has."

"He likes Madeline."

"I can see that," I said. "Who woulda thought."

"Yeah." She put her hand on my arm. "Let's join them on the dance floor."

After the song ended, Suzanne got back up on the microphone.

"Thanks for coming, everyone," she said.

Big cheers sounded in the room and my heart thumped, but in a totally good way. What a group. What a night.

"I'm thinking this should be an annual event," said Suzanne.

With that suggestion, the happy thumping slowed. I wouldn't be here next year. At Best Buddies, that is. High school would be over. Neither would Anna. She'd definitely be somewhere else. And maybe I would just be *doing* something else and not *going* somewhere else.

Emily dragged me out of my thoughts. "Thanks again," she said, "for letting me join in tonight."

"You're welcome. I hope you come to our next meeting. I'm not sure we can find you a buddy this year but you're more than welcome to come to our events. The group will need new members next year." I thought about Madeline. Maybe Emily could be her buddy next year.

"I'd love that," she said. She glanced over at Madeline. "We're going to go to a movie next week." She looked at her watch. "I have to head out so I'll go and say goodbye to her."

At nine o'clock, parents started showing up and suddenly Madeline lost her happy face and became agitated.

"I haaave to geeet goooing," she said.

"I'll walk you out." I didn't want her to face her mother alone, not with Becky gone.

Some parents were coming into the room to pick up their kids. They *oohed* and *ahhed* over the decorations and seemed thrilled that it had been such a success.

"You looked like you were having fun," I said to Madeline as we walked out to the lobby.

"I waaas."

"I'm happy Harrison asked you to dance."

"Heee's niiice," she said.

"I'm glad." I glanced at her out of the corner of my eyes. And I thought I saw a little smile on her face. Did she like Harrison?

"I liiike that heee taaalks soooo theeen I don't haaave tooo." She almost giggled.

157

"You do fine in the talking department."

"Thaaanks," she said shyly.

"You guys should do something together one day. Go to the movies— or I've heard he loves the science centre."

She laughed. "Buuut he's sooo smaaart."

I put my hand on her back. "So are you. You write poetry. You're amazing with animals. Maybe Harrison could go to the barn with you too."

She looked up at me, her eyes gleaming. "Are yooou coooming tooomorrow?"

"I sure am," I said. "I think my mother is too."

"I liiike your mooom." She paused and looked to the lobby. "Uuuh oooh," she said. "Theeere's *myyy* mooom."

Her mother walked through the community centre lobby, and when she saw us she waved. We waved back. She wore a huge smile on her face, and moved quickly toward us.

As she approached us, her smile turned into a beam. "Madeline," she said. "That video was amazing." She gave Madeline a big hug.

"Thaaanks," said Madeline.

"I wish you'd told me you were reading that poem. I would have stayed to watch."

"Theeere weeeren't ooother paaarents heeere," said Madeline.

"Okay. I guess I understand." She bobbed her head when she talked. "Well, at least Becky got to see it." She glanced around. "Where is she?"

She turned back to us. "Is Becky in the restroom?" Her eyebrows were almost touching.

Madeline shook her head.

"Where is she?"

"Sheee leeeft," she said, before I could answer.

"She left? How? Why? When?"

Madeline shrugged.

Her mother stared directly at me. "You *let* her go?"

"I'm sorry," I said. I wanted to say I didn't see her leave but that was a lie. I had seen her and I had tried to stop her but probably, maybe, not hard enough. Was I supposed to run after her? Was that my job? I deflated like a balloon.

"It's nooot his faaault," said Madeline.

"This is crazy," said her mother. "I dropped her off here. I assumed she'd be looked after."

"Mooom, sheee sneeeaks out aaat hooome too!"

"What?"

Madeline looked at the floor.

"Madeline, look at me."

Madeline looked up.

"What are you talking about?" her mother asked.

Suddenly, Madeline started to shake. Like, really shake. She clenched her hands. Her body stiffened. To date, I'd never seen her explode but Mrs. Beddington had told me her inability to control her emotions was part of her brain damage. And, I'd heard about some of her fits through other kids, like Gloria. From what I'd heard, sometimes they came out of nowhere. I wanted to reach out to her but I didn't know what I was supposed to do.

"It's okay, sweetie," said her mother softly. "We can talk in the car. Or at home."

"Sheee leeeaves laate at niiight!" Madeline yelled. And now, she was trembling from head to toe. She unclenched her hands. And gulped in air. She kept gulping.

Her mother put her hands on Madeline's shoulders. "Madeline it's okay."

"I caaan't heeelp it!"

"*Shhhh*," said her mother. "Where's Becky when I need her?"

"Sheee's nooot heeere!" Madeline screamed. Then she started hitting her head.

For a second I just stared but then I remembered. My sister, Faith, used to do the same thing when she was frustrated. "Madeline," I said quietly. as I gently grabbed her by the wrist. "It's okay. Breathe — but slowly."

She stopped hitting herself and slowly inhaled a huge breath before she blew it all out.

"Again," I said.

This time she breathed with control, and when she exhaled I could see her shoulders starting to relax. Three more times and she was calmer, but now she was almost too subdued, like she'd been given a shot of something. Her shoulders sagged and her body looked like jelly. I wanted to take her in my arms and hold her, like I used to with Faith. But I knew that would be a no-no in front of her mother.

She exhaled one more time before she looked up at me. "Thaaanks," was all she said.

"It's okay," I said. "I understand."

"Yes, thank you," said her mother, quietly.

"My sister was autistic."

"I'm sorry," said her mother. "Madeline told me what happened to her."

Now it was my turn to stare her mother directly in the eyes. She needed to know all the details I could give her about Becky. "I'm sorry that Becky left. I think she might have gone to a party. Cassandra's sister came and picked her up."

"In a car? Who's Cassandra?"

"Um, yeah in a car. Cassandra is a girl in her grade. Her sister is in my grade."

She took Madeline's hand. "Madeline, I think we should go."

As they walked away from me, I heard her say, "I'm sorry this has happened. You must be so proud of your poem."

I stood, watching them leave, and then I sighed. How could such a great evening have such a crappy ending?

CHAPTER FIFTEEN
MADELINE

"Would you like to dance?" Harrison asked.

The sparkling disco ball was going around and around, making lights shimmer and shine.

"Okaaay," I said.

Inside, my stomach bubbled, but in a really good way—effervescent, like soda bubbles. Not like when I was going to have a fit. It felt happy.

On the dance floor, Willa and Gloria were dancing with someone from the other school.

"Look how good I am," said Willa. She spun around.

"I'm not going to spin," said Harrison. "It will make me dizzy."

"Meee neitheeer. I miiight faaall."

Lots of other people were on the dance floor and Harrison moved over to the side a little. I understood that he didn't like crowds. The disco ball flashed up above, shining on all of us at different times. Marcie and Dan were dancing too, but Dan was just kind of running around, like he always did. Then he started dancing with Erika, and Marcie danced with Gianni. The song ended and "Y.M.C.A." came on. It was an old one but everyone knew it.

I did the actions the best I could, and tried to yell out the words at the right times. So did Harrison although he got the hand motions all mixed up and didn't yell. Erika changed it up by making her arm movements like a hip-hop dance. I laughed and danced.

After that song was over, Harrison said, "Thank you for the dance,

Madeline. I thought you did quite well, considering you have brain damage."

"Thaaanks. Yoooou tooo."

"I am starting to perspire so I think I would like to take a break. That is why I don't play sports although I'm also quite uncoordinated."

"Sooo aaam I." I laughed and Harrison actually smiled.

"Perhaps we could dance again at a later time," he said, "after I have had a soda. Although, I am not supposed to have *too* much soda. It is hard on my bladder."

"I'd liiike to daaance aaagain."

Emily came over to me and said, "That was fun." She glanced around. "I haven't seen your sister in a while. I wanted to meet her."

"Sheee leeeft," I said. I tried not to show what my insides felt. That she didn't want to be around me and my friends. But then, I didn't want to be around her and her friends either. The thought of that made my heart fall to my toes.

"I waaanted yooou to meet heeer too," I said.

"She's in my English class."

"Sooo you knooow her?"

She shrugged. "Sort of. We kinda don't have the same friends."

"Yeaaaaah. Saaame heeere."

The rest of the evening was perfect, and then it ended. The music got shut off and the lights came on. I didn't want to go home. I didn't want to tell my mother that Becky was gone. Again.

Justin walked me out and that's when I saw my mother. *Uh oh.* I started to shake before we even got to her. She walked toward me and I saw the smile on her face.

At first everything was okay because she gushed about my poem and told me she wished she could have heard me. My shaking and pounding head slowed a little. But then she started looking around in all directions and I knew exactly what was coming.

She turned back to me and started asking questions about Becky. I didn't want to answer her. Once again I started shaking. And this time it didn't stop. The barrage of questions made me hot and clammy. I could feel my heart beating. Faster. Faster.

Then she snapped at Justin. "You *let* her go?"

Why was she blaming him? Why? I didn't like that she was talking to Justin like that. My head pounded a steady beat. "It's nooot his faaault," I said.

"This is crazy," Mom said to Justin. "I dropped her off here. I assumed she'd be looked after."

"Mooom, sheee sneeeaks out aaat hooome too!"

Uh oh. Now I'd done it. I looked at the floor, at the scattered flecks on the tiles. I tried to relax my shoulders. Breathe. Unclench my jaws. Breathe.

More questions.

I didn't want to be asked these questions. I didn't want to answer them. I'd had a good night and now Becky and my mother were ruining it. Becky wasn't even in the room and she was wrecking everything. My body continued shaking and heat flowed through me. My heart was beating like crazy, sending the blood racing through my veins.

Don't freak. Don't freak. Not here. No. Please. Not in front of my friends.

"It's okay, sweetie," said my mother. "We can talk in the car. Or at home."

I didn't want to talk now!

And I didn't want to talk at home!

"Sheee leeeaves laate at niiight!" I yelled. Suddenly I couldn't breathe. Couldn't breathe. I gulped and gasped for air.

My mother put her hands on my shoulders. "Madeline, it's okay."

"I caaan't heeelp it!" And I couldn't. I wanted to. I did. I did. My body kept shaking. My head kept pounding.

"*Shhhh.* Where's Becky when I need her?"

"Sheee's nooot heeere!" I screamed. Then I started hitting my head. And hitting and hitting. I wanted to stop. But I couldn't.

Justin put his hand on my wrist. "Madeline," he said quietly. "It's okay. Breathe — slowly."

I stopped hitting myself and inhaled and exhaled. I kept breathing, slowly. In and out. In and out. I stared at the floor not wanting to see anyone looking at me. My cheeks burned in shame.

"Thaaanks," was all I said. I kept staring at the floor while Justin and my mother talked. I could hear their voices but I didn't really listen to the words. I concentrated on breathing. Not freaking. Calming myself down.

Then my mother took my hand. "Madeline, I think we should go."

Exhausted, I mumbled a goodbye to Justin, then held my mother's hand as I walked out with her. She nattered on about Becky and how proud of myself I must be. Really?

Proud.

Proud?

I had just freaked out in front of everyone. All anyone would remember was me having a fit.

Why couldn't I control my emotions? My brain. That' s why. *Stupid, stupid brain.*

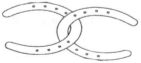

The tires squealed as my mother drove out of the parking lot. I leaned my head back, wiped out and still so mad at myself that I refused to talk in the car.

"Are you okay?" my mother asked.

She was driving so fast, I was getting sick. *Vertigo* they call it. I get it a lot since the accident. "Slooow dooown," I said.

"I'm sorry." My mother pressed her brakes a bit, and I breathed a sigh and slouched lower in my seat.

"Are you okay to talk about Becky?"

"Nooot reeeeally," I muttered.

"Has she really been sneaking out?"

My mother stopped at a red light and glanced over at me.

I knew she wanted some sort of answer so I nodded because I didn't want to waste my energy talking.

"You didn't tell me?" Her eyebrows were almost touching she was frowning so much.

I shrugged.

"None of this is your fault," she said, starting to drive again. "I'm not mad at you. I just want some answers."

"It's nooot Juuustiiin's faaault eitheeer," I said.

"You're right. This isn't Justin's fault. I promise I will apologize to him. I was just so taken aback. I don't know what to do. Should I go to the party and try to find her? Or just wait for her to come home?"

"Caaaall Daaaad."

"I can handle this." Then she muttered, "I think."

"Sheee miiiight gooo to hiiis hooouse laaater."

"Is that what she said?"

"I diiidn't talk to heeer. Buuut sheee waaants to liiive with hiiim."

"First I've heard about that," she said, sharply. "I seem to be the last one to know a lot of things."

I glanced out the window at the darkened streets, the leftover dirty snow, and the muted streetlights.

"Diiid you reeeally liiike my poooem?" I asked.

"Oh, honey, it was amazing. I'm sorry *your* night has come to this. I'm glad Becky sent it to me and your dad."

"Sooometimes sheee dooes niiice thiiings," I said, staring out the window again.

"Yes, she does." My mother sighed. "Sometimes I wish she would talk about things more, like about what's bothering her. About the accident, even."

Becky never, ever talked about my accident. She wouldn't. And whenever she came home from the therapist she would be all quiet. Years ago I had heard Mom and Dad talking about how she wouldn't talk with the therapist either. But she was always there to help me. She spoon-fed me. Took me to the bathroom. Encouraged me to walk. She made me repeat words.

Suddenly my stomach started doing flip flops and hurting: I was scared something bad was going to happen to Becky. Like, really scared. I pulled out my phone. Maybe Justin would know where the party was? I sent him a text. And I waited. Usually, he texted me back right away.

Finally, it pinged. He said he didn't know but would try to find out. I sent him a message back to say thanks.

I'd had such a good night and now it was terrible. I felt the tears and didn't want to cry but they started anyway.

"Madeline, honey, are you crying?"

"I hooope sheee's oookay." I sniffled.

"Me too. Are *you* okay?" She asked.

"Yeaaah," I said. These tears were different. I wasn't just having an out-of-control cry, I was actually really sad, in my heart, like it was split in two. Becky was my sister, my identical twin. Was I hurting because she was somewhere hurting? That used to happen to us. We knew when the other one was hurting, physically and emotionally. I wanted Becky to be okay and I wanted the night to stay happy.

"Leeet's just tryyy Daaad," I said.

Using the Bluetooth, Mom called Dad.

"Hi," she said quickly. "It's Leah."

"Leah? What's up?"

"Is Becky there?"

"No. I literally just walked in the door from my trip. I wasn't expecting to see the girls until tomorrow."

"Okay."

"What's this about?"

"Becky left Madeline's event at the community centre and has gone to some party. An older girl picked her up in her car but I don't know where they went."

"Oh no."

"Hiii, Daaad," I said.

"Hiya, Madeline. I loved the video of you reading your poem. You did a fantastic job!"

"Thaaanks." It kinda seemed like my reading was ages ago.

"Becky was the one who sent me the video," said Dad. "I just assumed she was there."

"Me too," said my mom. "But when I went to pick up the girls, she was gone."

"Why don't you two go home and call me when you get there? I can meet you at the house. We can come up with a plan."

"Juuustin might knooow wheeere the partyyy is," I said.

"That's a start," said my dad.

"We'll talk in a bit. See you at the house," said Mom and ended the call.

"Your father is right," she said. "We should get home in case she shows up."

We drove the rest of the way home in silence. The only thing I noticed was the time. 9:37. And the temperature. Just below freezing. Hopefully, there would still be enough snow to take the sleighs out tomorrow with the horses. I couldn't wait to see them. I thought about Tonya. She had asked to see my poem about the horses but I hadn't wanted to show her. But now, maybe I should show her. She had wanted to put it in her newsletter.

When we pulled up in front of the house, I saw a lump on the grass. "Mooom, looook!"

My mother squinted and peered out the front window of the car. Suddenly, she swerved and turned in the driveway. But instead of going into the garage, she shoved the car in park and jumped out. I opened my car door too and tried to get out as fast as I could. On my first step I almost tripped but I held onto the car and steadied myself. I moved quickly over to the grass. One foot in front of the other. One foot in front of the other. Faster. Faster.

"Becky!" My mother kneeled down beside her and gently tried jostling her.

Our front porch light was on, but Becky was lying crumpled up in a ball, in a darkened area on our grass. She moaned when my mother shook her.

"She's alive," said my mother.

I kneeled down too and smelt cigarettes and alcohol. Of course, I knew the smell. Alcohol was a regular thing in the girls' bathroom at school.

"Wheeeeere am I?"

"She's drunk," said my mother, sitting back on her heels. "Really drunk." She looked across Becky's body at me and the whites in her eyes lit up the dark. They looked more afraid than mad.

"Yuuup," I said. "Sheee is druuunk."

"I hope she doesn't have alcohol poisoning." Mom looked around. "How did she get home?"

"Beeeecky," I said, touching her on the shoulder and shaking it a little.

"I wannna shleep." Her eyes fluttered but didn't open.

"It's a good sign she can talk," said my mother. "She's not unconscious. Let's get her up and in the house."

"Okaaay," I said.

"Come on, Becky," said my mom. "Let's try and stand up."

"I'm sorrrrry," said Becky.

"You should be," said my mom.

"I'm sorrrry to *Maddie*." She tried to point at my mother. "Nnnot you."

"I dooon't caaare," I said. "Juuust tryyy and geeet up. It's cooold ooout."

My mother grabbed Becky under the armpits and lifted her to a standing position. I stood on her other side and let her lean against me. We started to walk forward but her legs were really wobbly. I had a hard time holding her up.

"Ooone steeep," I said. "Theeen the ooother." Just like Becky used to say to me when I was re-learning how to walk.

The front steps were a bit of a challenge. My mother held onto her but she stumbled and fell, hitting her shin against the edge. I thought she would react in pain but she didn't. She just fell forward.

"Oouuch," I said.

"Oh, she'll have a few bruises tomorrow," said my mother. "And a splitting headache."

We managed to get Becky into the house before she slumped over again, her chin falling onto her chest, her hair hanging in front of her face. Her body was like one big ragdoll.

"I think the best thing for her would be to get her to the sofa," said my mother. "Or on a chair."

"Yooou should caaall Daaad."

"I will. As soon as we get her lying down somewhere."

"Cooome on, Beeecky," I said. "Yooou gooot to help uuus."

"I wanna go to bed," she said, her eyes now droopy. I could sort of see her pupils. Her black eyeliner and mascara had run in black lines down her cheeks. What a mess.

"Maaaybe weee should taaake her to beeed," I said.

"I worry about her throwing up," said my mom.

"I caaan sleep in heeer roooom" I said. "Ooor she caaan sleep in miiine."

"Right now, she isn't your responsibility."

"M-m-addie," mumbled Becky. "I'm s-shorry." She almost spit when she talked, drool slipping from the side of her mouth to run down her chin.

"Stooop saaaying that," I said. "I dooon't caaare that you leeeft. I haaad a good tiiime wiiithout you." After my accident, we'd promised each other that we would still talk about everything, including boys. I'd had my first dance with a boy and I couldn't talk to Becky about it because she wouldn't even understand what I was saying.

"Thas nnnot whudda meant." She tried to open her eyes and look at me.

"Fooorget abooout it," I said. "Iiit's nooot impooortaaant."

"Yessit...is."

"Becky," said my mother. "We need to get you to bed. Up the stairs. We need you to help us do that so just stop with the sorry bit. We'll talk in the morning."

Mom and I managed, with great effort, to get Becky up the stairs and into bed. With every step, she grabbed onto the railing, her body swinging back and forth. We didn't bother to undress her, but we did take off her shoes. Mom said it didn't matter if she was in pajamas or not. She just needed to sleep it off.

"I'll siiit with heeer," I said.

"I'm going to call your dad."

Mom had just left the room when Becky rolled over and mumbled, "I'm gonna barf."

She tried to sit up but she swayed back and forth and then she flopped back down on the bed and just threw up. All over the sheets, her duvet and one of her stuffed animals that she still kept on her bed.

"Groooss," I said. It stank so badly that I held my nose with my fingers for a few seconds.

Becky didn't even notice the stink. She flopped back down, right into the barf. So disgusting.

"Mooom," I yelled.

Footsteps sounded on the steps and it sounded as if my mother was taking them two at a time. She rushed into the room, her phone up to her ear. Then she said into the phone, "She just threw up. All over the bed."

She stopped talking but she nodded.

"Yeah, for sure," she said. "I should go and clean this up." She paused. "No, it's okay. I can handle it. Madeline's been a huge help."

More silence.

"I'm not sure," she said. "She was mumbling about how *they* had dropped her off. I'm not sure who 'they' are." She ran her hands through her hair, sighed, and looked over at me. "I'll talk to Madeline." She nodded. "I agree." She sighed again. "I'll talk to her in the morning." A pause. "Yeah, I would appreciate your help."

That was the longest my mother had talked to my dad in a long time. I'd split them up. Was Becky putting them back together?

My mom changed the bed sheets while I sat with Becky in the bathroom. I sat on the edge of the bathtub and Becky sat on the floor with her face planted into the toilet. She barfed and barfed and I leaned over and held her hair so it didn't get completely covered in puke.

Finally, she lifted her head and I wiped her mouth with a wet hand towel. Then I rinsed it and wiped her face.

"Th-thanks," she muttered. "I n-need to go back to bed."

I helped her stand, grabbing hold of her arm. I almost lost my balance when she leaned into me, the weight of her body like a bag of bricks pushing against me. But I righted myself before I fell into the tub.

"I'm s-soorry."

"Stooop saaaying thaaat." I really was tired of her telling me she was sorry. She went out and got drunk and I had a great time at a dance. Whatever.

I had written in my poem that we were different even if we were from the same egg and that was becoming more and more apparent every day.

"I am s-s-sorry," she said *again*. "Everything is my f-f-fault."

Then the drunken waterworks started, just like on TV. Drunk girls always cried. Tears streaked down her face, and snot dripped from her nose. I held onto her and managed to walk her back to her room. My mom had finished changing the sheets. She held pajamas in her hands. "Let's get her undressed. I don't want her sleeping in her own vomit."

"Sheee puuked tooons," I said. "I triiied to wiiipe her faaace."

"You did a great job. And it's actually a good thing that she vomited when she did. Kids have died from puking in their sleep."

While we got her in her pajamas, Becky kept saying she was sorry. Over and over and over and over. I tried to ignore her because the repetition grated on me, banging against my head. I didn't want to have another fit. I tried to breathe. In and out. In and out. The word *sorry* just kept circling around my head. And the leftover smell of puke didn't help much.

"Are you okay?" My mother eyed me.

"Sheee keeps saaaying the saaame thing."

"You go, honey. You've helped enough. I can do this."

"I thiiink I'm fiiine nooow." I wanted to handle this.

"I've got things covered," said my mom. "You go take a break."

I nodded. Heat seeped out of my pores. I could feel it. I did need to remove myself from the situation.

With Becky still babbling about being sorry, I left the room and went downstairs to get a drink of water.

I was staring out the kitchen window when I heard my mother's footsteps. She gently touched my shoulder. "Can I make you something to eat? Maybe a bowl of popcorn? We could watch a TV show or a movie."

"I'm nooot huuungry," I said.

She turned me to face her and lifted my chin. I stared into her eyes. "It's been a long night for you. Pretty emotional too. You've had a lot of ups and downs. But you really need to focus on the ups, okay? Your poem was amazing. You have lots of friends."

"I wiiish I diiidn't have a fiiit in frooont of myyy frieeends." I lowered my head.

She pulled me into her arms and hugged me. I leaned my forehead against her and started to cry. Again, they weren't drunk tears or fit tears. They were real tears.

"Don't cry, honey. If they're your friends they won't care. They will understand."

CHAPTER SIXTEEN
JUSTIN

"I just got a text from Madeline," I said to Anna. We had gone for coffee with the organizers from St. Frances to discuss the evening event, what worked and what didn't. Mostly it had all worked. Now we were almost at my house. I'd been worried sick about Madeline and Becky the entire time I was at the coffee shop.

Yes, Becky. I had let her get in that car.

"Did they find her at the party?" Anna put on her blinker and turned down my street.

"No," I said. I looked down at the phone and read the text aloud, word for word.

Found Becky drunk on our lawn.

"On the lawn? Are you kidding me?"

I fired a text back.

How did she get there?

I waited for a few seconds until I heard the familiar ping.

dropped off?

"Madeline thinks she was dropped off," I said.

"Really?"

"Yeah, pretty bad, eh? I bet those girls just got her drunk and dumped her."

"Some friends." Anna turned into my driveway, and right away I noticed that lights shone from inside. Someone was up. The light wasn't on in my parents' bedroom. I sat there thinking for a few seconds. Mom had been better and staying up a little later, not sleeping so much all the time. *Should I?* I didn't want my night with Anna to end so soon.

"You wanna come in?" I blurted out. "It's early. Only ten."

"Are you sure?" Anna leaned forward over the steering wheel and stared out the front window of the car at my house. I saw her gaze shift upwards. "I wouldn't want to disturb your mom if she's sleeping."

Rarely did I invite Anna into the house. Usually, we spent time at her place. But lights were on. That was a good sign. *Could I hope?*

"Yeah," I said with forced confidence. *Could I? Should we?* My confidence fizzled. "I guess I could text my dad first."

you up??? I hit send.

He sent back a happy face and a checkmark. I laughed.

"What are you laughing at?" Anna furrowed her eyebrows.

I showed her my phone. "My dad thinks he's so cool."

"Too funny. But I would think he means yes."

"My mom's been a lot better lately." I opened the car door and a rush of cool air greeted me. I liked it.

Anna also got out but she grumbled. "I wish spring would hurry up." She looked over at me. "Do you think your mom is better because of those little horses?"

I walked around the car. "Maybe," I said. "Fresh air, horses, Madeline. All of that. Madeline has been wonderful with her."

We walked hand in hand up my walkway. Even from outside, the energy of the house felt better, seemed more alive.

"You've got a bounce in *your* steps," said Anna.

"It's been a good night despite the Becky situation. Now that she's home and safe I can breathe. And lights are on! That's such a good thing."

"It was a good night," said Anna, squeezing my hand. "I feel bad for Madeline though. After such a fantastic start, I bet she's upset with how it ended."

"She can't help having those fits," I said.

"I know," said Anna. "I wonder if they're worse right now, at her age, because of hormones?"

I shrugged. Leave it to Anna to try and figure out the medical reason. Her brain just moved that way instinctively.

I opened the front door and heard voices. The hall light was on. The kitchen light was on. A warm air flowed from the heating vents. But best of all was the smell of popcorn.

"Yum," whispered Anna.

We both slipped out of our shoes and headed into the kitchen. My dad stood at the counter and my mother sat on a chair at the kitchen table. She wore jeans and a sweatshirt and her hair looked shiny and clean. Almost like my mom used to look, except for the bags beneath her eyes, and the yellowish tinge to her skin. But she looked better—so much better. I would take better any day.

"Did you save some for me?" I asked.

My dad held up the bowl. "Nope." His laugh rang through the kitchen, almost as if he was a giddy teenager. "But I can make more." He looked over at my mom. "You game for more, Lori?"

She waved her hand. "I'm good but make some for the kids."

Kids? Did I hear her correctly? She called us *kids*?

If she was going to stay up, I was going to eat popcorn. "I can make it," I said.

"I can help," said Anna.

My mom smiled a little bit at Anna. "So nice to see you, Anna."

"It's good to see you too," replied Anna.

"I heard you're on your way to California," said my mother. "You must be excited."

I understood my dad's giddiness. Inside I was feeling the same thing. I'd told her about Anna's plans for university, but didn't really expect her to remember and make it part of an actual conversation.

"So excited," said Anna. Her eyes always shone when she talked about going to university. I put the popcorn in the air popper.

"It's good you're following your dreams," said my mom. She paused. I turned to see her playing with her cigarette package. "Justin has to figure out where he's going."

"I'm getting there," I said.

She lifted her head and gave a little smile. "I'm sure you are. You always were decisive as a little boy. And when you made your mind up, you made your mind up."

"I think," said my dad, "this might be the first time Justin has been confused about anything."

I held up my hands. "Enough about me."

My mom pointed to the air popper. "Make your popcorn."

I turned the machine on and the noise drowned out any conversation. Soon, the kernels started exploding, and fluffy white popcorn spilled out into the bowl. Anna put the butter in the microwave. Once it was made and salt added, we joined my mother at the kitchen table. Although there was awkwardness, it was okay. One step at a time.

My father brought over a deck of cards. "Let's play a card game."

I waited for my mother to bow out but she didn't.

"What should we play?" I asked, seizing the moment, afraid to let it go.

My mother lasted thirty minutes playing cards then she begged off, had a quick cigarette outside, and went to bed. My dad whistled as he cleaned up the kitchen.

"I should get going," said Anna.

"I'll walk you out."

Once outside, I peered up at the night sky, at the stars blinking, and I heard Faith's voice in my ear: *Go for a walk.*

"You wanna go for a quick walk?" I asked Anna.

"Sure," said Anna. "It's a beautiful night."

Anna linked her arm in mine and we walked down my street, the night air cool, refreshing with a light breeze.

"Your mom seems so much better," she said softly.

"Yeah. I hope it holds. She's still smoking though."

"Right now, I would say that's the least of her worries. Give her time to get used to the world again." She giggled a little. "I liked the stories about you when you were a little boy."

"So embarrassing."

"Nah. Cute."

"Ha ha. I'm anything but cute."

She squeezed my hand. "Even if you decide not to go to school next year, you should try and keep your marks up for the future. There's still time to work and study." She bumped me with her hip. "I'm a heck of a tutor, y'know." Then she stopped and spun me to face her. She gave me a sassy smile. "And I won't charge you, except a kiss now and again."

I looked into her dark eyes and saw them shining, just like the stars in the sky. "How about now?" I whispered.

I liked the feel of her lips on mine, and heat flowed through me. I pulled her closer and she responded. How long did we kiss on the street? Who knows? Who cares? Not me that's for sure.

Afterward, we stood holding each other. Then suddenly the brisk air returned, and Anna started shivering.

"You're cold," I said. "Should we go back?" I rested my cheek on her hair, loving the silky feel, the sweet smell.

"I can't wait until summer," she snuggled into me, resting her cheek on my chest. "Then we can just stay outside all night long and enjoy every minute."

A rock fell to the bottom of my stomach, almost as if I'd been punched in the gut. I wanted to agree with her but I knew with summer came fall again. And that's when she would go and I would stay. Our days would be numbered in the summer.

"I don't want time to go by too quickly," I whispered.

She pulled back and looked up at me again. "I believe in us," she said.

I nodded and we started our walk back to my place and her car. "So…I've been thinking of going to community college next year," I said. "Just take a few general classes, and just get a job and live at home for the year. And I'd like to continue volunteering for Tonya. Then I'd get to see Madeline too."

"That's a plan," she said. "And that's a good start. Any idea what kind of job?"

I shrugged. "Whatever I can get, I guess."

"Fair enough," she said. "Why don't you look for a feel-good job? Maybe at a non-profit organization?"

"Yeah," I said. "Maybe."

She stopped walking to look upwards. "Oh wow! Look at that."

As she pointed, a little white light was flashing through the sky.

"Where'd it go?" Anna kept staring up.

I started to laugh.

"Why are you laughing?" She nudged me with her shoulder.

"This is going to sound totally crazy but…that shooting star is Faith. She's playing with me."

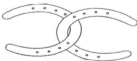

I awoke before my alarm, something that hasn't happened to me in years. Sun streamed through my window, making straight lines on the carpet. It was sunny outside and I felt a certain sun in my soul—some sort of brightness, lightness, like maybe I didn't have to be miserable all the time.

If the sun was shining then it would also be melting the snow, I realized. No more sleighs. I should help Tonya put them away. I peeled myself out of bed and put on my barn clothes. And, like my dad last night, I started whistling.

I almost bumped into my dad in the hallway. He was up and dressed and whistling too. He laughed. "We should start a father-son whistling duet."

"Um, okay," I said. I laughed with him. "There's a problem with that though because neither one of us is really all that good."

"Is Mom up?"

"She sure is. And dressed for the barn."

I went downstairs where Mom was sitting at the table, drinking a cup of coffee.

"Hi, Mom," I said.

"Good morning, honey. Did you have a good sleep?"

"Great sleep," I said. I went to the coffee pot and poured myself a cup. "How about you?"

She shrugged. "Better. Nights are still hard."

I nodded. I knew she took sleeping pills but I didn't want to ask if she was still taking them. I didn't want to talk about that kind of stuff. Not this morning when the sun was shining and the birds were chirping and there was this lightness to the air.

"I'm looking forward to seeing the horses," I said. "And Madeline too. I have a feeling Tonya is going to need help putting the sleighs away."

"Faith always did better in the spring," said my mother. "I'm going to try too." She stood up. "I'll tell your dad we're ready to go."

CHAPTER SEVENTEEN
MADELINE

S un peeked through the blinds in my room. I rolled over to see that it was already nine o'clock. I inhaled a deep breath and tried to think about last night. Today, my brain felt like a slow computer logging on to the internet. I had to wait for it to boot up and tell me what had happened the night before. When I was tired, it took longer.

I glanced at my phone. Saturday. Barn day. I looked at my chair. All my barn clothes were there. I didn't remember putting them out. Foggy, foggy brain.

I laid still and tried to remember the night and, piece by piece, some of it started to come back to me. The good and the bad. I closed my eyes for a moment and saw small snippets of the dance; the conga line, Harrison asking me to dance. Then a dark cloud rolled over all the good stuff. Had I really freaked? I buried my face in my pillow. My stomach turned.

Then I thought about Becky. I got up and went into her room. Her bed was a crumpled mess and she was sprawled out, still sleeping. I went over to her bed and sat down, glancing around at the black t-shirts and jeans marking the floor. Then I smelt the leftover alcohol and vomit. More memories floated through my fog. She'd been drunk all right.

"Beeecky," I whispered.

No movement.

"Beeecky," I said a little louder.

She rolled over and faced the wall.

Obviously, she didn't want to get up yet. I stood and went back to my room. I sat on my bed. I was tired.

A little knock sounded on my door.

"Madeline," said my mom. "Time to get up."

"You caaan ooopen myyy door," I said.

The bedroom door creaked and Mom stood at the doorframe all dressed and she looked like she was in her clothes that she wore to the barn. She hadn't been to the barn in months. She glanced over at my chair and she pointed, "I put out your clothes last night."

"I caaan dooo it," I said.

"I know," she said. "But when I checked on you last night, I noticed you hadn't done it yet. Which is understandable, considering the night we all had."

I narrowed my eyes. "Are yooou coooming wiiith meee?"

"Is that okay? I thought it might be refreshing to be outside this morning."

"Suuure," I said. "Is Beeecky coooming too?"

"Dad is on his way over. He will bring her. He wants to talk to her alone."

I picked up a calendar I had beside my bed, telling me if I was at my mom's or my dad's. It was dad's turn to pick us up after being at the barn. "Aaare weee still goooing to Daaad's todaaay?"

"That's the plan."

I nodded. "I'll geeet dreeessed," I said.

Once I was dressed in my barn jeans and barn sweatshirt, I headed downstairs for breakfast. My mom had made French toast and bacon, which was weird for her because she usually saved it for special occasions, but I wasn't going to ask questions. I liked French toast and I loved bacon.

As usual, I didn't talk a lot when I ate, and I was halfway through my breakfast before my mother finally spoke. Most meals she nattered on and on and asked a million questions that were usually directed at Becky and not me. She usually didn't ask me many questions for fear that I might choke.

When she did finally speak, she said, "Tell me more about last night. *Your* night."

Shocked that she didn't ask me about Becky, I pointed to my mouth (since I had food in it), and she nodded, waiting for me to finish chewing. When I did, I said, "It waaas reeeally fuuun."

"That's it?" She tried to smile at me.

"I duuunno," I said. "We daaanced and diiid this cooonga thiiing."

"A conga line? Cool."

Sometimes my mom quizzed me in the morning to make my brain work. Usually it made me cranky, but today it was okay. I wanted to remember dancing. I paused and picked up a piece of bacon with my fingers. "Aaand a phoooto booth."

"Did you take any photos?"

I nodded. Then I popped a small piece of bacon in my mouth.

"Can I see them?"

The photo was in my jacket pocket. Again, I nodded and pointed to the mud room where my jacket was.

"Okay, show me later," she said.

When I finished chewing and swallowing, I remembered something and said, "I waaanna gooo to a mooovie with Emiiily on Suuunday."

"Is Emily the friend from science class?"

I nodded.

"A matinee would be fine," she said. "What movie?"

"*Staaar Pooower.*"

"I've heard that's good," said my mother. "I'd like to meet Emily."

After all that had gone on with Becky and her mysterious new friends, I had no problem with that. "Sheee's niiice," I said.

My mother played with her food, pushing it around her plate. "Madeline, I'm sorry about last night," she said. "You shouldn't have been dragged into all that happened. And I shouldn't have blamed Justin for Becky's actions. I said I would apologize and I will this morning."

"It's oookay," I said. "I freeeaked ooout."

"Forget about that," she said. Then she stood and started clearing the breakfast table. "It's over. This is a new morning and we're going to get some fresh air."

I took my plate to the dishwasher too.

"We'll leave in five," said my mom.

Our car ride was silent and I appreciated that. I stared out the window at the sun shining in the sky, warming the ground. There was barely any snow and whatever was left was melting. Puddles were already forming on sidewalks and the road. I looked forward to spring and walking the horses through green grass. I wanted to ride the big horses again. Maybe I could ask for lessons for my birthday.

When we arrived at the barn, there was a police car in the parking lot and Tonya was talking to two police officers. Her face looked all scrunched up like she was crying.

"Oh my goodness," said my mother.

"Whyyy wooould the pooolice be heeere?" Something wasn't right. I could see by the look on Tonya's face and how she was waving her arms around.

"Let's find out," replied my mother. She parked the car and we got out.

Tonya saw us, said something to the police, then ran over to our car. Her boots sloshed in the mud. Her jacket flapped against her side with every step. There was this wild look in her eyes. I'd never seen Tonya look like this before.

"What's wrong?" my mother asked.

"I don't know what happened," she cried. "Some of the horses are gone!"

"Gone?" my mother asked.

Gone. I stared at her.

Tonya was crying and almost hyperventilating she was breathing so hard. "Someone…someone must have l-l-let them out in the night."

"Iiis Wiiillooow gooone?" My voice wobbled.

"Willow *and* Cowboy. Whoever did this also took one of the sleighs." She put her hand to her chest. "They're my babies. I can't lose them."

Willow. Cowboy.

They couldn't be gone. They couldn't be. I wouldn't let myself think that. I just wouldn't.

I reached over and hugged Tonya. "We wiiill look fooor theeem," I said. And I meant it. No matter what, I was going to do everything I could to help.

"We'll all help look," said my mother.

Tonya went back to talk to the police as a car came up the road, and when I saw it was Justin and his mother, I waved furiously and walked over to meet him.

"Sooomeooone leeet the hooorses out!"

"What?"

"Wiiillow's gooone!" I wanted to cry but I didn't. And I wanted to freak out but I didn't. "Cooowboy too."

Justin took my arm and we headed over to Tonya and the police, followed by his parents.

"What happened?" Justin asked.

"When I got here this morning," said Tonya, "the corral doors were wide open. Someone had jimmied the lock and either they've stolen the horses or freed them." She stopped for a second and put her hand on her chest again and she breathed. "I'm sorry. My heart is out of control."

"Have you looked in the woods?" Justin's dad asked.

"Not yet," answered the police officer.

"I was here last night in between 9:00 and 9:30 and I made sure everything was locked and they were all in their stalls." Tonya added. "Someone must have come after that."

My stomach churned at the thought of someone hurting Willow and Cowboy, coercing them out into the snow for no good reason. "Weee need to looook," I said. "Iiin the fieeelds."

"And woods," said Justin.

"Why wouldn't they come back?" Tonya moaned.

"We should split up," said Justin.

"If you are going to search," said the police officer, "and you come across something that looks like evidence or a crime scene, please don't touch anything. Just let us know right away."

"Okay," said Justin, his voice shaking.

"Someone needs to stay here," said Tonya. "Parents are going to be arriving soon." Tonya tried her best to hold back tears but they still trickled down her face. "This farm is all about helping kids. How could someone do this?"

Heat started to race through me. I could feel my head pounding. I couldn't freak, lather, whatever. I just couldn't. I breathed in and out to relax. I let my arms fall to my side. I unclenched my fingers.

I had to do this.

Then I heard Justin. "Mom, are you okay?"

I turned to look at Lori, and that's when I noticed that her face was as white as fresh snow. She stared into space with a blank look on her face.

Justin glanced quickly at his dad who nodded and put his arm around Justin's mom. "It's okay," said Justin's dad. "We'll find them."

"Yeah, Mom," said Justin, his voice higher than normal. "We'll all look."

I walked over to Justin's mother and took her hand in mine. "Weee wiiill fiiind theeem," I said.

Lori hugged me. And I hugged her back. I could feel her body trembling, just like mine.

I moved away from her and turned to look at everyone. "Leeet's spliiit up and staaart lookiiing."

Justin nodded. "Madeline's right. The sooner the better."

I looked at Tonya. "Whyyy dooon't you staaay at the baaarn. Theeey miiight cooome back."

"We have a few more questions for you too," the police officer added.

Tonya nodded.

Justin's dad squeezed his mother's shoulder and asked her, "How about if we look together?"

I looked over at Justin. "Caaan I look wiiith *yooou*?"

"Absolutely," he answered.

"Why don't you stay near the barn with Tonya and the police, Madeline?" my mom said quickly. "I can go with Justin."

I turned to my mother. "Juuustin and I wooork weeell tooogeeether. Yooou staaay with Tooonya."

My mother tilted her head and stared at me for a second. But then, to my surprise, she said, "Okay. You and Justin go. I'll stay here."

Justin and I worked at splitting everyone up and figuring out who would look where. His dad and mom were going together to search the perimeter. Justin and I would go deeper into the woods. My mom was going to stay with Tonya and help her out as the other parents arrived, which I thought was a great idea.

Justin and I headed toward the wooded area. I walked slower than I would have liked but the path was uneven. One foot in front of the other.

Please, please, just let them be wandering around and not stolen or worse.

"Theeey're oookay," I said, trying to convince myself.

"I hope so," Justin said.

"Wiiillow!" I called out. "Heeere, preeetty giiirl."

No whinnying answer. No sound of movement. No soft neighing. We kept walking until we hit the edge of the woods, then Justin spotted a pretty good trail.

"Let's take this trail," he said. "Tonya did tell me there is a pond back there. They might be drinking water."

"Wiiillooow!" I kept calling her name as we headed onto the trail. "I haaave caaarrots!"

I looked side to side, and through the tree branches, hoping she was just caught on one somewhere. It was easy to see because the buds had yet to appear and the branches were bare and dry. Then it hit me. What if we did find a *crime scene*?

I couldn't let myself go there. "Cooowbooy!" I called out. "Wiiillooow!"

We kept walking deeper and deeper until we came to the pond. I'd never been back this far on Tonya's five-acre property. The fence was broken in places and Tonya had said she was saving up to repair it one day.

I was so hoping to see both horses, lapping at the water, having a drink, totally unaware that a bunch of people were worried sick. But they weren't there. The sun-dappled water shone, and little ripples floated across the surface.

"Are you okay to walk around a bit?" Justin asked me.

"Yeees," I said. I put my hand on his arm. "Buuut juuust stoop for a seeeecond."

He stopped and stood beside me. I closed my eyes. I could feel her. I really could. Willow was near me. I tried to listen for her whinnying but all I heard were the branches rattling in the wind. I opened my eyes. "I knooow she's heeere sooomewhere."

Justin inhaled a deep breath and blew out air. "I know. We can't give up," he said. "My sister is telling me not to."

"Doooes sheee taaalk to yooou?" I asked, peering up at him.

He shrugged. "I'm not sure if she talks to me or if I just want to hear her voice."

I nodded. "Thaaat maaakes seeense." And it did. I cupped my hands around my mouth and called out. "Wiiillow! Wiiillow giiirl! Cooowboooy!"

"Willow!" Justin called out too. "Cowboy!"

We walked a little farther around the pond and we came to a little clearing. Then I saw it.

Right in front of the water sat the sleigh, toppled over and trashed. I moved toward it and when I saw the mangled runners, I felt sick. How could someone have done this? Why wreck something for no reason?

Justin swore under his breath.

I saw black burn holes on the vinyl cushion.

Justin pointed to cigarette butts that littered the dirt. Then I saw the crumpled package. Camel cigarettes. That's what Becky and her friends smoked. My stomach soured.

"I can't believe this," said Justin.

"Beeecky's frieeends smooke thooose," I said.

"So do lots of people. We need to tell the police about this. And leave it alone, like they said." He pulled out his camera and took photos of the sleigh and the cigarette package.

Yeah, lots of people smoke this kind, *including my twin sister.* I stared at the ground. Suddenly, I saw something glistening in the dirt. I eyed it for a second. It looked familiar. I bent over and saw a black feathered earring. Filthy and matted, it could have been mistaken for a real bird feather but the glistening metal part of the earring had caught my eye.

"Thaaat is Gwiiinnie's," I said, pointing.

Justin scowled and snapped a close up of the earring. I focused on my breathing. In and out. I had to keep my emotions controlled. I just had to. *Please, brain, please.*

I wondered how they'd got the sled out here. There must have been more than one person. I walked over to the bushes and started pushing them aside with my feet. And, of course, I found alcohol bottles.

"Someone definitely had a party," said Justin, looking down at the ground at the empty bottles. "Tequila and rum." He took more photos. "We should probably go tell the police what we found."

"Nooot yeeet," I said. "Weee neeed to fiiind the hooorses."

"You're right," he said. "We've come this far. Let's keep looking."

"I hooope they diiidn't huuurt...theeem."

Justin quickly turned around to face me and put his hands on my shoulders.

I looked at him. "Fooorget I saaaid thaaat." I stood tall again. I was going to save Willow and Cowboy. I had to. They had to be alive.

We continued along the trail until we hit some brambly bushes. I stuck my hand in to try and get through and felt the prick of the thorns. I yanked it back and saw the blood trickling on my wrist.

"Don't go that way," said Justin.

I turned around and I was walking away from the bushes when suddenly I heard something. I stopped walking and closed my eyes.

And listened. And listened.

Was it a whinny?

"Are you okay, Madeline?" Justin asked me.

I put a finger to my lips. "*Shhh.*"

I stood completely still. At first I only heard the wind rustling through the bare branches and the pond water moving back and forth to the rhythm of the wind. I just moved my head slightly, trying to tune into the sounds.

Then...I heard the little neigh! *Again.* I did. I heard a neigh. But it also sounded like a soft moaning. Willow had heard me too! She was calling me.

"Thaaat's heeer!" I started running toward the bramble bush. I didn't care if I got cut. I didn't. I didn't. I had to find her.

Justin chased me and pulled on my jacket.

"Don't go in that way," he said.

"I haaave tooo."

"No." He scanned our surroundings and pointed to another trail. "We can go over there. It might be a bit longer but we should get to the same point."

We hurried to the trail, which was better marked. The feeble neighing got louder and louder. My heart quickened, making my pulse go faster and faster. I had to move quickly, but stay calm and not trip.

Yes, I had to stay calm. One foot in front of the other. One foot in front of the other.

"I can hear her, Madeline!" Justin exclaimed. "You were right! I can't believe you heard her."

We came to a little opening and a steep hill. It wasn't a big hill but it was muddy with small snow patches dotted here and there. We both stared down.

There at the bottom of the hill stood Willow, her mane tangled in a bramble bush.

"Wiiillow!" I cried out. I started to move down the hill but Justin grabbed onto me.

"It's steep," he said. "And slippery."

I shook my head. "I'm goooing. She neeeeds meee."

I got on my butt and slid down the mud toward Willow. When I got to the bottom, I stood up, not caring one bit that my butt was soaked. Justin sidestepped down the hill.

I rushed toward Willow.

"Wiiillow," I said in a low, soothing voice. I scratched her nose and leaned in to her. "Dooon't worry. Weee'll get yoooou freeee."

She looked at me with total trust, then whinnied and nudged her nose against me.

"Yooou're oookay," I whispered. "I wiiill free yoooou."

CHAPTER EIGHTEEN
JUSTIN

The bramble bushes were covered with prickly thorns. Strands of Willow's mane were caught in the bushes, and she couldn't move.

"Weee haaave to beee geeentle," said Madeline.

"Agreed," I said.

Madeline got down on her knees and gently pulled one strand of Willow's mane. She slowly tugged and tugged until it was free. I watched in awe for a few seconds. I'd never seen this take-charge side of her. She definitely had it in her.

I kneeled down as well. "We can do this," I said.

She nodded but didn't stop working. Strand by strand we released Willow's mane. The prickly bush cut our hands and blood dotted the snow below the bramble bush. No matter how much Madeline bled, she just kept working.

The coarse mane felt somehow soft. The entire scenario felt surreal. The wind blew gently through the trees. Birds chirped around us as if to say, "Keep going."

Madeline had this magic touch. Somehow, she worked to free Willow and scratch her nose and stroke her neck and kiss her. All at the same time. Oh, and feed her carrots.

"It's oookay, Wiiillow," she said. Over and over. The horse calmed.

It took time but together we got the job done. Finally, we had Willow free.

I sat back on my heels. Madeline wrapped her arms around Willow.

"I tooold you. Yooou're oookay." She nuzzled her nose into Willow's neck.

Willow neighed.

"Now we have to get her up the hill," I said. I so hoped there was nothing wrong with the horse. Drunks could do stupid things. I thought about how one of Becky's friends had said how fun it would be to ride the horses.

"Cooome on, Wiiillow," said Madeline.

The little horse moved and I watched her carefully. She seemed to be okay. Resilient, like Madeline. Willow started up the hill. Madeline used Willow for support.

Madeline held on to Willow and the little horse held her up as if she knew Madeline needed help climbing the hill. I followed behind Madeline in case she slipped. We moved slowly and steadily, and soon we were at the top of the hill.

"Not much further now," I said.

I have no idea how long it took us to get into the clearing but when we did I held up my hand and Madeline slapped it.

"We did it," I said. And the best part is she's okay."

"I neeeed to ruuub soooomething on heeer cuuuts," she said, leaning down and tenderly rubbing her fingers over a couple of the scratches on the side of Willow's belly.

My hands were bloody and scratched but Willow had scratches all over her body.

"Beeecky did thiiis," she said.

"We don't know that for sure," I said.

"Yeees. Weee. Dooo."

"You found her at home just after 9:30," I said. "And Tonya said she was here with the horses until almost 9:30."

She thought about that for a second before she said, "Sheee brooought thooose giiirls heeere."

"You start walking to the barn," I said, glancing around. "I'm going to take a quick look around for Cowboy."

She nodded and started leading Willow back toward the barn.

I called Cowboy's name, and searched a bit, but when there was no answer, I jogged to catch up to Madeline. We both kept calling for him as we made our way back.

Then, when we got close to the ring I saw Cowboy and my dad.

"Heee's saaafe toooo!" Madeline almost squealed.

"Yeah!" I cheered.

Then I glanced around and saw Madeline's mother. I also saw my dad but not my mom. Maybe she was in the barn, getting the stalls ready? Madeline's mom must have seen us coming because she pulled at Tonya and pointed to us.

"Hallelujah!!!!!" Tonya raised her arms in the air.

"Hey, Madeline." I pointed to the ring. "Four horses—they're all here."

"The sleeeigh is still broooken, though," she said angrily. "Beeecky ruuuined it."

I glanced at her. Her face was drawn and pale, but her eyes were defiant. I understood. All was forgotten when we were trying to save Willow but now that she was okay the fact that Becky was maybe, perhaps, sort of, involved stared us right in the face.

As we approached the ring, Tonya and Leah rushed right over to us.

"You found her!" Tonya leaned down and hugged Willow. "Oh, Willow. You poor baby."

"Sheee neeeeds oooint...meeent," said Madeline struggling with the word a bit. She was tired, I could tell. "Sheee haaas scraaatches. Frooom aaa...priiickly buuush."

Her mother eyed her. "Are you okay, Madeline?"

Madeline nodded. Then she turned to Tonya. "I caaan taaake her. Ruuub heeer."

"Okay," said Tonya. "I would really appreciate that."

"The sleeeigh is broooken."

"My sleigh?" Tonya narrowed her eyes. "Where is it?"

"In the clearing," I piped up. Madeline had done enough talking. "By the pond. I took photos for the police."

"That sleigh was a *gift f*rom a little girl's great-grandmother," said Tonya. "She'd seen how the therapy had helped her granddaughter and she wanted to give back. It was a beautiful antique and perfect for here."

"Maybe it can be fixed," I said.

She straightened her shoulders. Then she said, "Doesn't matter. What matters is all the horses are here."

"Iiis Beeecky heeere?" Madeline asked.

"Not yet," said Madeline's mother. "But your dad texted and said they were on their way. I didn't say anything to him about any of this yet."

"Where did you find Cowboy?" I asked, changing the subject.

"He was just near the edge of the property," said Tonya, "but he's fine."

"Did my mom and dad find him?"

"Your mom helped for a while but I think the stress got to her a little bit. She decided to sit in the car. Your dad found him not long after."

My throat felt as if it was being choked. *Not again. Please.* She was doing so well. "Okay," I said, trying not to show how upset I was that my mother didn't want to look for the horses. I hoped it wasn't the beginning of another setback.

A car sounded in the parking lot and we all turned to see who was arriving.

"There's Dad and Becky now," said Leah to Madeline.

Madeline stiffened. I wanted to tell her to take Willow to the barn, go rub her cuts, heal her, because she could, she had a magic touch. But I didn't think she would listen.

Madeline hugged Willow and said, "I'll beee baaack to heeelp you."

With slow and steady steps, she started to walk toward the car. Leah went to follow but I said, "Maybe you should let her go."

She turned to look at me.

"There's something you should know," I said. "Madeline found something by the sleigh."

CHAPTER NINETEEN
MADELINE

Becky.

Suddenly, my head hurt, and the pounding pressed against the sides of my skull, but this head pain felt different. I was mad. My twin sister had ruined a beautiful sleigh and almost killed two horses. Well, pretty much. She had brought those girls to the barn. Last night she kept telling me she was sorry. She must have known what they were going to do.

I walked across the field toward the parking lot. I stumbled. Once. Twice. But I kept moving. Three times. My heart pounded. And pounded. My mouth felt dry and I wondered if I would even be able to speak. Sweat trickled down my face. My muddy pants were heavy on my body. I didn't care. Then I heard footsteps behind me.

"Madeline!" my mother called out.

No way. She wasn't going to stop me. Not this time.

Of course, she caught up to me. She tried to pull my arm, get me to stop, but I yanked it away from her. And almost fell. She held onto me to keep me from falling.

"This is not the way to go about this," she said.

"Whaaat iiis the waaay?" I kept walking. I looked down at my feet, willing them not to trip me, send me falling flat on my face.

"Madeline," my mother caught up to me.

"Leeeave meee."

"I don't want you to be getting upset." She walked beside me. "We don't even know if Becky was the one who was here."

"Theeey aaare *heeer* frieeends."

"Madeline, try to calm down."

I stopped walking, turned, and glared at her. "I'm maaad. Oookay? NOOOT haaaving a laaather. Aaaas you liiiike to saaay."

I started walking again. I saw Becky with Dad and she was wearing an old light green jacket of hers. Not black. And a baseball hat. She used to always wear baseball hats. Was she trying to pretend something? Dress the part of old Becky, nice Becky, so she would not have to pay for what she did?

"Hey, Maddie," she said. Her face looked tired, her eyes were bloodshot, no eyeliner today, and her skin was sort of grey. And she looked sheepish. I knew that look. I remembered that look from when we were little and she'd gone in my room and taken Halloween candy, or when she'd stolen my bell off my bike and put it on hers because she had taken hers apart and ruined it. When I'd had the accident, she didn't have the bell on her bike because I'd made her put mine back on my bike. That was the last thing I remember from before my accident. She had broken her bell like she broke everything.

I didn't answer Becky. Didn't say hello back. I stared her right in her bloodshot eyes.

"Whyyy diiid yooou leeet the hooorses ooout?"

"The horses?" She tilted her head and pushed her eyebrows together. "What are you talking about?"

"Yooou kneeew the hooorses weeere out!" I screamed. "Gooot druuunk and leeet the…hooorses ooout. Hooow coooould yooou…" My brain struggled to keep up with my words. And I struggled to breathe. I wheezed and tried to gulp air. "…saaay nooothing?"

"It wasn't me," she protested. "Honest! I wasn't anywhere near the horses last night."

"Theeey broooke Tooonya's sleeeigh." Tears fell down my cheeks.

"What is going on?" my dad asked.

"Someone let the horses out last night," said my mother. "And took one of the sleighs."

"Wiiillow haaas scraaatches. The sleeeigh is wreeecked. Caaamel cigaaarettes weeere byyy the sleeeigh and Gwiiinie's eeearring." I'd talked so much my words were coming out like my battery was dying.

My mother put her hand on my shoulder and gently squeezed it. "Madeline, it's okay."

"Iiit's noooot!"

"Becky couldn't have been here," she said. "And this anger isn't good for you."

"Whaaat's nooot good fooor meee iiis *heeer!*" The ends of my fingers started to pulse. My body trembled. Heat surged through me like a burning fire. Pounding. Pounding. I lifted my hand to hit my head but then I reached out and slapped Becky across the face. She reeled backwards, holding on to her cheek.

I gasped and pressed my hand to my mouth.

Becky looked at me, her eyes full of hurt.

Why had I hit her? I didn't mean to hit her. I really didn't. I'd meant to hit myself.

My body started to tremble. Then it shook. The pounding started inside my head.

I had hit her instead of me. I wanted to hit myself. I did. I couldn't though. Otherwise it would all be about me and my brain. No one would get how mad I was at Becky. Confusing. Confusing. I shook my head.

"I wasn't here last night," Becky sobbed. "I really wasn't. I was...in... the park."

"With who?" my mother asked.

"Cassandra and her sister and her friend. And Gwinnie and Molly too. You have to believe me."

Everything started swirling inside of me. My head ached. Pain pounded against my skull. I felt dirty and hot and sweaty. And tired. Really, really tired. I caved and sank to the ground.

Becky came over to me and kneeled down beside me.

"Leeeave meee," I said, without lifting my head.

"I wouldn't hurt the horses. You have to believe me, Maddie. When I left your event last night I went with them but...we went to the park. They made me drink shots. I got so drunk I pretty much passed out and they drove me home."

"Buuut you brooought them heeere. Yooou shooowed them this baaarn."

I tried to stand up. When Becky went to help me, I moved away from her and managed to stand up by myself. "I'm goooing tooo...to the baaarn."

"I can help you," said Becky. "Please."

"I waaant to be alooone."

As I started to walk away, I heard my father say, "Leah, leave her. Let her be alone."

I got to the barn and Tonya met me and pulled me close to her. "Are you okay, sweetie?"

It felt good to have her arms around me because I knew she loved the horses as much as I did. "I waaaanna see Wiiillow."

She patted my back before she pulled away and lifted my chin. "I've got the ointment ready. She's waiting for you. And patiently I might add."

Willow was in her stall even though it was day and she whinnied when she saw me coming. The ointment was on the shelf where Tonya said it would be so I picked it up and went into her stall. I wrapped my arms around her neck.

"I'm sooo sooorry. I'm goooing to fiiix yooou uuup."

She blinked at me.

Rubbing the ointment in Willow's scratches helped me calm down. When I heard the footsteps on the floor, I didn't look up and kept applying the ointment.

"Hey, Madeline," said Justin softly. "How are you?"

"O-kaaay."

"Do you need help?"

I nodded.

He came into Willow's stall and pulled up a little foot stool and sat beside me.

"Whaaat tiiime waaas Tonya heeere laaast niiight?" I stared at the hay on the floor.

"Until around 9:30. Everyone discussed it outside and Becky couldn't have been here."

"Buuut heeer frieeends weeere."

"Probably. But no one knows that for sure."

"Diiid sheee knooow? Sheee keeept saaaying sheee was sooorry."

"I don't think she knew anything. She might have been saying sorry for something else."

I carefully rubbed ointment into one of Willow's scratches. Justin helped. Willow whinnied, telling us she enjoyed the extra special treatment we were giving her. We didn't talk anymore. I was all talked out.

After a bit, I'm not sure how long, I heard more footsteps and turned around and saw Becky and my parents.

"Dooo youuu neeeed tooo geeet goiiing?" I asked Justin. "Wiiith Yooour paaareeeents...?"

"Nah, they already left. I'll catch the bus," he said with a shrug. "I can wait with you."

By now my parents and Becky were at Willow's stall. My father must have heard Justin because he said, "One of us can drive you."

"It's okay." Justin stood and brushed hay off his pants.

"No, I insist," said my dad. "It's the least we could do."

I gave Willow a hug and a kiss and said, "I'll beee baaack on Weeednesdaaay, oookay, giiirl?"

She blinked at me and whinnied.

"I waaant to go hooome," I said.

"Do you want to come with me, Madeline?" my mom asked.

"Iiisn't it Daaad's tuuurn?"

"I don't think it matters today," said Dad.

"I'll gooo wheeerever Beeecky iiisn't goooing."

"Becky is coming with me," said Mom.

"I'll gooo wiiith Daaad."

"Maddie, please," said Becky.

"Nooo." I brushed by her and headed out of the barn and straight to Dad's car. Outside, the air had shifted and it was sunny, and there was a warm spring breeze. Dad followed me and so did Justin. I got in the front seat. Justin got in the back even though he insisted that he could take the bus.

Dad drove and none of us talked for most of the ride home. I stared out the window at the patches of brown grass and the puddled sidewalks. People walking, biking, looking happy. Justin only spoke up when he had to give my dad directions to get to his house.

My dad pulled up to the curb and Justin tapped me on the shoulder. "Madeline, if you need to talk, call me," he said.

I nodded.

When the back door had slammed shut my dad said, "He seems like a good kid." He pulled back onto the road and I watched Justin walk in his front door, hands in his pockets. He looked as sad as I felt.

"Heee's niiice to meee," I said.

"You've had quite a weekend." Dad glanced at me sideways as he drove.

"Beeecky ruuuined iiit." I traced my finger along the window.

"I'm sorry about that."

"It's nooot your faaault." I paused to think, letting my words catch up to me. I knew what I wanted to say. The words were in my brain and I just had to let them form. After at least a minute I said, "Sheee wants to liiive wiiith yooou so…she caaan go…ooout at niiight."

"I think your sister is turning a corner. She learned a few things last night and we had a good chat this morning." He quickly took his eyes off the road to glance at me. "She really is sorry."

"Reeed liiight." I pointed to the light ahead.

He stopped. "Your mother and I need to spend more time with her," he said. "With both of you."

The light turned green and he started up again. "We thought we could go for dinner tonight," said my dad. "Just the four of us. What do you think about that?"

"I need aaa baaath," I said. "Aaand I waaant tooo sleep."

CHAPTER TWENTY
JUSTIN

Madeline walked away, heading to the barn. Her mother went to follow her but her father told her to leave her alone.

"Mom, Dad," said Becky. "You have to believe me. I wasn't here." The girl was crying, sobbing actually.

I didn't really want to listen to Becky's crying but I also didn't want to go to the parking lot and see that my mom was a mess or that my dad had driven her home. So I just stood like a lump. I had brought my mom here only to make her spiral down again.

"You need to give the names of the girls to the police," Becky's father told her.

Her mother held up her phone. "I need to show them these photos that Justin sent to me."

Even though I felt as if I was intruding on a family altercation I was stuck to one spot, my feet refusing to budge. Becky had her arms crossed over her chest, almost hugging herself.

"If I tell *you,* can you give them to the police?" Becky almost whispered.

Her father sighed. "Okay, I'll go talk to them first, since we don't even know if it really was those girls. Right now we're all just making assumptions." Her father put up his hand. "But, Becky, if the police want to ask you questions, you will have to talk to them."

I looked at Leah. "I'll stay here with Becky," I blurted out. "If, um, you want to go too."

"Thank you, Justin," said Leah. "I might go see if Madeline is okay."

After her parents were out of sight, Becky turned to me, but barely met my gaze. Droopy eyelids covered her puffy red eyes. Her skin was red and blotchy from crying. And no doubt she was hungover.

"I really don't know anything," she mumbled.

"For what it's worth, I believe you. Timing is wrong. But I'm not sure it wasn't your friends."

She lowered her head again and looked at the ground. Then she kicked dirt with her foot. "They're not my friends anymore."

"Why *were* you hanging out with those girls?"

The tears stared up again, rolling down her face, and she pressed her hand to her mouth, almost biting her skin.

Did I want to hear her answer? I wasn't even really her friend. And I certainly wasn't her psychologist. But maybe if someone had listened to me, I might not have gotten into a big fight and gotten kicked out of a school. "Seriously. It doesn't do any good to look for trouble."

"Okay! You want to know the truth?" She finally stared me right in the eyes. "I was the one. Okay. I was…the one." She pointed her finger at herself. Then she tapped it, over and over, harder and harder. I could hear the impact on her breastbone from where I was standing. If she didn't stop she was going to bruise herself. I reached out and took her hand.

Her body sagged. "I'm the one who ran my bike into Madeline's and she fell." Her voice was barely audible. "I didn't have a stupid bell on my bike. I took it apart. Broke it. And my wheel hit hers and she fell!" She started to hyperventilate, gasping in and out for air. "Her brain damage is my fault. My. Fault."

"Becky, relax." I put my hand awkwardly on her shoulder. "You were eight years old."

"They…they helped me forget. They had nothing to do with my old life before the accident. They were…different. But then they used me.

They turned on me."

"Nothing can make you forget," I said. "Trust me. I know."

I saw her parents coming toward us without the police and dropped my arm to my side.

"Here come your parents. You should tell them what you told me."

"Will they make me tell Madeline?" Her voice quivered.

"Talk to them," I said. "That's the best thing you can do. I'm going to the barn to check on Madeline."

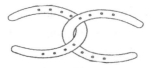

Inside the barn, Madeline was rubbing ointment on Willow. She was by herself. I approached quietly, so as not to disturb her concentration. I really didn't know if she wanted me to join her or if she still wanted to be alone.

"Hey." Even though I said this as quietly as I could, my voice seemed to echo in the barn. "How are you?"

She didn't look at me but kept working on Willow. "Oookay," she answered.

I went into the stall and sat down on a little footstool. I got that she didn't want to talk so we kept the conversation to a minimum and spent most of our time working on Willow. With everything that was going on, my role was to be Madeline's friend. And sometimes friends didn't need to talk, they just needed to be.

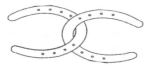

Madeline's father insisted on driving me home but it was the most awkward ride of my life. Madeline sat in the front and stared like a zombie out the window as her father tried to make small talk.

Finally, he pulled up in front of my dark house. No lights on.

"Thanks for the ride," I said when I got out of the car. "Madeline, if you need to talk, call me." Even if she didn't call me, I planned to call her later.

I walked in my front door and the grandfather clock chimed two. We'd been there all morning and I needed a shower. My shoes were caked with mud and my pants were filthy. I was sweaty, hot, and tired. At least the horses were okay.

But was my mother?

I went into the kitchen but not one light was on. "Dad," I said softly. No answer. I went to the bottom of the stairs and grabbed the wooden newel post. I only knew it was called that because my mother had told me. She had laughed about it and made me repeat it to her. *Newel post. Newel post.* That's when she was bubbly and funny and full of life.

I glanced up and dread seeped through me. Where was my dad? I needed him right now.

I headed up the stairs, my legs feeling like they weighed a million pounds each.

Outside the door of my parents' room, I stopped and listened. At first I heard all the white noise swirling around me but then...I heard breathing. The sound of life made me knock.

I heard footsteps coming to the door. My dad pushed it open and pressed his finger to his lips. I nodded and backed away from the door. My father tiptoed out and quietly shut the door behind him.

"How is she?" I asked.

"Okay," he said. But the half shrug he gave told me otherwise.

"Tell me straight up, Dad."

He put his hand on my shoulder. "It's just a relapse. That's all. The doctor told me this could happen. But, Justin, she has made progress. You have to know that."

"The horses," I muttered.

"She got overwhelmed."

"Should I cancel dinner with Anna tonight? Remember, I invited her over."

"No, have her come. I will still cook."

"She's bringing dessert," I said.

He smiled and patted my back. "I hope it's full of fat."

I playfully punched him in the stomach, and he playfully punched me back, and right there in front of the bedroom door, we jostled around, trying to make like things were normal, lighten the situation.

For a few seconds it worked.

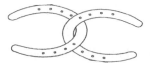

At six o'clock the doorbell rang and I ushered Anna into our front lobby, taking the plate she held in her hands. Whatever was underneath was covered in aluminum foil.

"Smells good in here," she said.

"My dad's cooking. It will be chicken and veggie-something-or-other. What's for dessert?"

"Cheesecake," she said. "I made it from scratch."

"Awesome," I said. "We'll probably need it to fill us up." I put the dish down on the counter. "Um, so, my mom might not join us."

"I'm sorry to hear that," she said. "The horse stuff just sounds awful. I don't have to stay, you know."

"It's okay. We want you here."

"How's Madeline?"

"She's so strong. She amazes me."

"She is strong. She's been through so much but she just keeps moving forward." Anna paused before she said, "Can you imagine being an identical twin? Having someone in the world who has your DNA and looks exactly like you? They came from the same womb and the same placenta even. They're the same but, yet, they're so different."

"They sure are."

We went into the kitchen and I showed Dad the cheesecake and he patted his belly and held up a bowl of cut vegetables. We laughed. Actually laughed. And all seemed sort of normal—missing a piece, but we were coping.

My dad put out a plate of appetizers, some shrimp on cucumbers, and we nibbled and, of course, the conversation steered to school. While Anna talked, I turned one of those small serviettes around and around on the counter, sort of mesmerized by the movement.

Then I heard my dad's voice. "You like those shrimp?" he asked.

"Sure do." I took one off the plate and popped it into my mouth.

"They're so good," said Anna. She took a shrimp and popped it in her mouth too.

"They're one of my favourite appetizers." My mother's voice startled us all.

In unison, we turned to stare at her, standing in the doorframe, her hair wet, her body clad in clean yoga pants and a t-shirt.

"Sorry, I didn't dress for dinner," she said.

I quickly got up. "No worries, Mom."

She held up her hand and motioned for me to stay seated. "Sit," she said.

"I'm glad you could join us," said Anna.

"Thank you, Anna."

My mother sat down on an empty stool and she took a shrimp and actually took a small bite before she put it on a serviette.

"Are you going to live on campus next year, Anna?" my mother asked.

She nodded. "I'm looking forward to setting up my room."

My mom turned to me. "I want you to go away too, if that's what you want to do."

"I appreciate that," I said. "There's only one problem. I don't really want to, not next year anyway. I have decided I want to take a year off to decide. I think it will help me make a better choice, in the long run."

My father patted my back. "That's my boy. Such a mature decision."

"Don't worry," I said. "I won't freeload off you. I'll get a job."

My dad held up his knife. "No freeloading allowed."

We all chuckled, a little anyway.

When the joke had died, my mother said, "Don't stay home for me."

"I won't," I said. "I'll do it for me. It's what I want. I need time to make a decision. What's one year?"

"One year is nothing," said Anna.

"In a year," said my mom, "I might be able to help you set up your dorm room." Her eyes twinkled for a second, before fading. But I saw it. I did. There was some life behind her eyes and if nourished it could grow.

CHAPTER TWENTY-ONE
MADELINE

At first I liked how quiet my dad's house was without Becky. I got out of my filthy barn clothes and took a long hot bath, using Becky's bubbles. Then I ate a ham-and-cheese sandwich and a bowl of hot soup that my dad made for me. Then I took a nap.

I woke up at 3:30, rolled over, and found the remote for the television on the night table I shared with Becky. I turned on the television and automatically asked, "Whaaat doooo you waaant tooo waaatch?"

Of course, then I looked over and saw crumpled sheets, a tossed duvet cover, but no Becky. I flicked through station after station, finally settling on a silly teen sitcom about a girl who sees ghosts at school, one of Becky's favourites. Mine too.

For over an hour, I watched brainless television, chatted briefly with Justin, and texted with Emily about what movie we were going to see, until my father knocked on my bedroom door.

"Cooome iiin," I said.

He opened the door and frowned when he saw Becky's bed. "Does she ever make it?"

"Nooo. Neeeither dooo I."

"Least of our worries, right? Look, dinner is at six. I'd like you to come."

At first when I came home, I said I wouldn't go. But I'd been in my room all afternoon, alone. Maybe going out wouldn't be the worst thing in the world.

"Okaaay," I said.

"We'll leave at 5:45." My dad smiled and shut my door. Leave it to my dad not to ask me why I'd changed my mind. We worked well together. I liked his lack of questions. Perhaps that wasn't good in Becky's case, though. Maybe he should ask her more questions, like Mom did.

Once again, I was alone in *our* room. I flicked through a few more stations then shut the television off and got off my bed for the first time in hours. Becky had all kinds of clothes in our closet and I started going through them. Black, black, and more black. Then I stopped and pulled a beautiful beige cable knit sweater from the hanger. She'd got it for Christmas from *me*. It still had the tag on it.

The sweater felt soft on my body when I put it on and I examined it in front of the mirror, liking how it fit. I wondered if I could try to do my hair like she had done it for me. I sat down on the floor, in front of the long mirror my father had bought at the discount home store when he was setting up our room. I turned the flat iron on and waited for it to heat up.

Awkwardly, I straightened strand after strand. In the end it looked okay but not as good as when Becky had done it for the party.

The party. Had it just been last night? It felt as if it was ages ago. For the first time in a long time I'd had fun, like a regular teenager. Until the end. Then I was back being the brain-damaged one who had a fit.

My phone pinged and I grabbed it. I smiled. It was a message from Harrison.

Thank you for the dance. I hope you are okay after your meltdown. That's what my mother calls it. I'm always quite tired.

I giggled.

me too

We should say hello at school.

ok. Monday

Yes. I would like that. Please be in the front lobby at 8:52.

With my phone in my hand, and a smile on my face, I went downstairs, deciding not to put on any makeup to go along with the hair. Dad glanced up at me when I walked into the family room, put down his paper, and gave me a thumbs-up.

"Nice sweater," he said. "Um, have you talked to Becky yet?"

I shook my head.

"She's going through a lot," he said. "She's sorry for a lot of things."

"Sheee alwaaays saaays sooorry. It buuugs meee."

"Maybe ask her why."

"Oookay. Weee'll see."

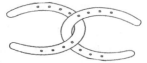

My dad and I drove to the pizza restaurant in our comfortable silence but when he turned off the car in the parking lot, he didn't get out. Instead he put his hand on my shoulder. "I'm hoping we can keep this pleasant."

"I miiissed heeer toooday."

"I'm glad to hear that," he said.

Mom and Becky were already seated when Dad and I walked in the restaurant. The hostess guided us to the booth. We were dining at an upscale pizza place that had what my mom said were the best thin-crust pizzas in the city and the best calamari.

"Hello," said my mom in this chipper voice.

"Hi," said Becky.

My dad took my coat and hung it up for me while I slid into the booth beside Becky. I didn't look at her. But when I reached for my water, she did as well. Our hands touched for a brief moment. Things like that happened to us all the time. Both of us pulled our hands back at the same time as well.

My dad opened his menu and glanced down. "So what is everyone having?"

"Maaargheriiita piiizza," we said together.

She nudged my shoulder and I sat there for a few seconds before I looked at her.

"I missed you at Mom's today," she said.

"I miiissed yooou too," I said. I took a sip of water.

"You're wearing my sweater."

"It stiiill haaad a taaag on iiit."

"It looks good on you but...I might want it back." Tonight, she was wearing one of her other beige sweaters. That happened too. We often picked out the same colour without consulting with each other. Well, before she started wearing black.

"Dooo yooou...stiiill waaant to liiive at Daaad's?" I asked her.

She slouched in her seat and eyed Mom. "Uh, I dunno."

My mother placed her menu on the table. "We need to talk about this."

My dad clasped his hands on the table and leaned forward a little. "I certainly don't mind more custody but you need to spend time at both our places." He paused. "Becky, look at me."

Becky breathed out before she looked up, but her chin was down and her eyes were droopy. She didn't say anything.

"I know you think if you come to my place you'll get to do what you want. But you won't. In fact, after all that has happened in the past few days, I will probably be stricter than your mom."

"I haaave sooomething to saaay," I said.

"Go ahead, Madeline," said my mother.

"I waaant us to staaay togeeether."

"Me too." Becky's voice sounded strangled. She put her arm around me and leaned her head on my shoulder. "That's all I want, Maddie. I want to be with you."

The waitress interrupted us. "Are you ready to order?" She pulled out her notepad and looked at Becky and me. Then she furrowed her eyebrows. "Are you twins?"

"Yeaah," we said together. Then we looked at each other and giggled. Her hair was still black and mine was blonde but we were definitely twins.

After we gave our orders to the waitress and she had left, my mom asked, "So, Becky, are you going to dye your hair back to its natural colour?"

She shrugged. "I actually kind of like it dark. It makes us at least a little bit different."

No one said anything for a few seconds. I guess we all had to think about that. Then Becky said, "Maddie, I have something I want to tell you."

"Iii'm liiistening," I said.

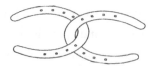

On Monday, I went to school and at lunch I met Justin in front of the cafeteria. We were just about to go into the cafeteria when Anna came up to us. Justin held up a package of cards.

"New game," he said. "Uno."

"Gooood," I said. "Eeemiiily miiight join uuus."

"Great," said Justin. "Uno is a better game if you can play it with more people. I used to play with my grandmother."

We found a table at the side of the big noisy cafeteria and sat down. I had just pulled out my lunch, when Emily sat down with us too. "Oh my goodness, Madeline. I just read your poem again. It's so good," she said.

Justin winked at me. "I hope you don't mind but I sent it to her and to Tonya. She's putting it in her next newsletter. If you agree that is."

My face flushed. But in a good way. "Thaaaat's oookay," I said. And it was better than okay. I was happy.

"That was such a good movie yesterday," said Emily, biting into her sandwich.

"I loooved iiit," I replied. And I *had* loved it, especially the medieval horses in it. When I got home, I'd talked to my mom about taking proper riding lessons and she had said that perhaps I could start in the spring. Real horse-riding lessons!

"What are we playing?" Emily asked.

Justin held up the cards. "Uno."

"Oh, I love that game. I play it with my family."

Justin had just dealt the cards when I saw Becky walk into the cafeteria, alone, dressed in black jeans but a green shirt. She'd gone halfway. Her head was down, her hair hanging in front of her face. Who was she going to sit with? I saw Cassandra and Gwinnie get up when they saw her. Like two mean crows, they walked over to her. When they got near her they bumped into her on purpose, made a rude gesture, and pushed their way by her.

Becky stood by herself. A sharp ache pressed against my heart. Becky had given their names to the police and in the end Molly had caved. Or that's how Becky had put it. She said she was the only one with a heart. Molly told the police they'd taken the sleigh for fun, and let the horses out by mistake. I didn't believe Molly for a second. They had *taken* the horses out on purpose. I don't think Becky really believed her either. Tonya still had to decide if she was going to charge them with vandalism.

"Beeecky," I called out.

She glanced over and I waved. A look of relief spread across her face and she walked over to our table.

"Hey, Becky," said Justin.

"What are you playing?" She hugged her books to her chest.

"Uuuno," I said.

"You want to join us?" Emily asked.

"Sure." She sat down beside me.

Our right thighs, upper arms, and shoulders touched, joining us together.

I looked at her.

She looked back at me.

I held up my pinky finger. She smiled at me and hooked her pinky finger in mine.

"Beeesties," I whispered.

ACKNOWLEDGEMENTS

I am so thankful to so many people who helped me as I wrote this novel. Peggy Lalor, my friend since we were both nineteen and living in Banff. You were always such a fabulous athlete, from jumping waves in Maui to skiing double black diamonds. You went through so much after your bike accident and you never gave up. I have watched you work, day after day, to learn how to eat and walk and talk. I remember my trips to visit you at the Halvar Jonson Centre for Brain Injury in Ponoka, Alberta. You inspired me to create Madeline, a character with a zest for life, even after tough times.

Thanks to Anne Marie de Jong at the South Okanagan Brain Injury Clinic for answering my questions and giving me insight into Madeline.

I'm also extremely grateful to Patty Harris Seeley for introducing me to miniature horses. You knew that putting me to work, even shovelling poop, would make my story better. I loved being at your barn and being introduced to Daphne, Cher and Cowboy. Yes, I named three of my fictional horses after your horses. I love what you're doing with these little gems, as they help so many kids and adults.

To Clockwise Press...thank you, thank you. You ladies are so incredible. Christie, your edits are truly amazing. Your sense of what works and what doesn't astounds me, and I'm so appreciative that you make my story better. Solange, your business sense is awesome. (Note I didn't use the word amazing!) And your final edits always pick up those little stragglers.

And now to my readers. I LOVE YOU! Thank you for reading my series, for telling me you love my characters, and for embracing diversity! Please enjoy!! I love Justin and Madeline and I know you will too.

ONE-2-ONE SERIES
also by Lorna Schultz Nicholson

FRAGILE
BONES
HARRISON & ANNA

Lorna Schultz Nicholson

ISBN 978-0-99393-510-7

ONE
★2★
ONE

BORN
WITH
ERIKA & GIANNI

Lorna Schultz Nicholson

ISBN 978-0-99393-517-6

CLOCKWISE
PRESS
www.clockwisepress.com